"Lukas!" she gasped, delight shooting through her body.

Lukas pulled back to look into the depths of her violet eyes, his gray ones smoldering with desire for her. "We should stop?" he asked her throatily.

She swallowed hard. She didn't want to stop. She wanted more of his kisses, more of his touch. "Do—we have to?" she asked.

Jessica Steele lives in a friendly English village with her super husband, Peter. They are owned by a gorgeous Staffordshire bull terrier dog called Florence, who is boisterous and manic, but also adorable. It was Peter who first prompted Jessica to try writing, and after the first rejection, encouraged her to keep on trying. Luckily, with the exception of Uruguay, she has so far managed to research inside all the countries in which she has set her books, traveling to places as far apart as Siberia and Egypt. Her thanks go to Peter for his help and encouragement.

Books by Jessica Steele

A SUITABLE HUSBAND

Jessica Steele

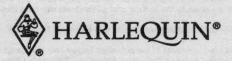

TORONTO • NEW YORK • LONDON
AMSTERDAM • PARIS • SYDNEY • HAMBURG
STOCKHOLM • ATHENS • TOKYO • MILAN • MADRID
PRAGUE • WARSAW • BUDAPEST • AUCKLAND

ISBN 0-373-03667-1

A SUITABLE HUSBAND

First North American Publication 2001.

CHAPTER ONE

IT WAS not unusual for Jermaine to work late. She was part of the sales support staff at a busy plant and machinery manufacturers and was used to working under pressure. Her work was varied, but mainly she dealt with reports from Masters and Company's top-notch sales executives when they either rang in or visited head office in London.

This week she had nothing in particular to rush home for. It didn't matter that it was going on for eight o'clock when she let herself into her small flat.

She had been going out with Ash Tavinor for three months now, only for the last two weeks Ash had been working away from home in Scotland, too far away for him to return to London, or for them to spend any time together. He could have flown down, of course, but he preferred to work at the weekends, the sooner to get his business done.

Jermaine smiled as she thought of him. She had missed seeing his happy sunny face. She would be glad to see him again. He was tall, good-looking and—her smile dipped a little—had broached the subject a month ago of some kind of 'commitment' from her. In fact Ash had called her old-fashioned in the extreme, because she was not prepared for them to become lovers in the true sense of the word.

She had wondered herself, since knowing him, if it was time to yield her stand. The stand she had taken six years ago when her beautiful sister, Edwina, had clapped her eyes on Pip Robinson, Jermaine's first boyfriend, and decided that she'd like him for herself.

Jermaine recalled again the hurt she'd experienced then. She supposed she couldn't have been all that fond of Pip because it hadn't been his defection that had hurt so much. She had been more bruised by the fact that her sister— whom, it had very soon became apparent, had had no particular interest in Pip other than as another conquest— didn't care that he was Jermaine's boyfriend.

Suddenly Jermaine didn't feel at all like smiling. Pip hadn't been the only boyfriend Edwina had clapped eyes on and taken from her.

Jermaine made some coffee, musing that it wasn't any wonder that, over the years, her decision not to make the sort of commitment Ash wanted her to make had become deeper and deeper entrenched.

But her smile came out again; all that had been before Ash. Ash was different. When she had been going out with him for about a month, she had grown to like him so much that she had begun to ponder occasionally about introducing him to her sister and taking the risk of everything falling apart.

She had pondered needlessly. Ash had met Edwina and—nothing. Not that Jermaine had ever come to any decision about introducing him to Edwina. Neither of the Hargreaves daughters lived with their parents any longer. But Jermaine and Ash had been driving through the Oxfordshire countryside one early September afternoon when she had happened to mention that her parents lived close by.

'Don't you think it's time I met them?' he had teased, as ever smiling. She had smiled back—most men ran a mile at the thought of meeting a girl's parents.

She had tensed up, however, when, turning into her parents' drive, she'd seen that she and Ash were not the only visitors that Sunday afternoon. Edwina's sports car had been parked outside.

'My sister's here,' she'd informed Ash, and had hidden

her reluctance to go into the large old house she had been born in.

She need not have been concerned. Ash had been pleasant and courteous to her parents, and had smiled and been polite to Edwina, and that was all. Jermaine hadn't missed the way her sister had gone into action—the smile, the breathless laugh, the big blue eyes attentive, absorbed in every syllable Ash uttered.

Ash had been unmoved as Edwina had flattered his choice of car and enquired—after an interval—what sort of profession he was in. 'I'm in computer software,' he had answered, and, probably because he was proud of his elder brother, 'I work for my brother's company, International Systems—I don't know if you've heard of them?'

Edwina hadn't, but Jermaine hadn't doubted as her sister's glance had taken in Ash's discreetly expensive shoes and clothes, that she would soon be finding out all about the forward looking company—and its wealthy chairman—not to mention Ash, the chairman's far from impoverished brother. Edwina liked money. Regretfully, Jermaine realised, that had been one of the chief reasons for Edwina calling on their parents that afternoon: because her bank account could do with topping up. Their father thought the world of Edwina and, although Edwin Hargreaves's income had greatly reduced when the stock market had received something of a massive hiccup, Jermaine guessed that her father's cheque was already residing in her sister's purse.

Jermaine made herself some cheese on toast to go with her coffee, reflecting how more than two months had passed since that Sunday. It was now the beginning of December and, although she had since paid quite a few more visits to her family home—especially when her mother had gone down with flu—she had not again met Edwina there.

Jermaine's thoughts drifted to her parents for a moment

or two. She was aware that she was not her father's favourite, but her mother had always sought to be scrupulously fair to both her children. Though, thinking back, Jermaine realised her pain over the Pip Robinson business had caused her mother pain too. Even then, though, when annoyed at her twenty-year-old daughter's heartlessness, she had not remonstrated with her beautiful blonde offspring but had striven instead to bolster up the shattered confidence of her younger platinum-haired daughter.

'She doesn't want him!' Jermaine recalled complaining, vulnerable, shaken by Pip's behaviour and hardly able to believe her sister could have acted in the way she had. 'Just because she's beautiful...'

'You're beautiful too,' he mother cut in gently, much to Jermaine's astoundment.

'Me?' she'd gasped, conscious only that she was thin and seemed to be all arms and legs.

Grace Hargreaves had given her sixteen-year-old a hug. 'You,' she'd smiled, and, at Jermaine's look of surprise, 'You're losing that gangly look, filling out in all the right places. Give yourself another year and you'll see.' And when Jermaine hadn't looked convinced she'd added, 'Your complexion is flawless, match that with your lovely violet eyes and you're going to be outstanding.'

Jermaine had never known her mother tell her a lie, but wasn't very sure about 'outstanding'. 'You don't think the colour of my hair's a little bit weird?'

'Not in the slightest. Learn to love it,' her mother had urged. 'You really are a sight for sore eyes, sweetheart.'

Over the next couple of years, when her burgeoning curves had fulfilled their promise, Jermaine had come to accept and quite like her white-blonde hair. By that time, however, Edwina had used her wiles on any male friend her sister brought home, and it had soon become clear to Jermaine that, while there might be only four years' difference between their ages, there was a vast difference between their natures. She would never, and could not ever, behave in the way Edwina did.

Edwina had not been at all happy when her father's finances suffered a reversal—though not unhappy so much for him as for herself. Jermaine had been sixteen then, and had left school at once and got herself a job, but Edwina had no intention of working for a living. Her father had indulged her—she regarded it as her right.

Edwina was greedy but, when in sight of men, could be most generous if, by being so, it would get her what she wanted.

After another couple of boyfriends had succumbed to Edwina's charms, Jermaine had known that she was never going to commit herself to any man unless she was certain that he wanted her and nobody else. There was no way she was going to give herself or go to bed with any man until she was two hundred per cent positive that it was her, and her alone, that he wanted. She was just not interested in any fickle affair where her sister could waltz in, bat her big blue eyes, smile that particular smile kept for such occasions—and take over. Good grief! Jermaine came to with a start, realised she had finished her light meal without being conscious of having eaten—and wondered what on earth had sent her off into reflective mode of things past.

Ash and the commitment he wanted from her, very probably, she realised. But Ash was different. True, her own tastes had changed. She had moved on from the lightweight males she had been drawn to up until a couple of years ago.

She supposed it was all part and parcel of growing up. Two years ago the company she worked for had invited her to transfer from their Oxford branch to their head office in London. It had been a very flattering offer. To go had not been a difficult decision to make. Edwina, while returning home when it suited her, had already moved out several times. She had then, however, been back again, and was lazy, untidy and given to treating Jermaine's wardrobe as her own. Edwina was, in fact, generally a pain to live with, and at that time had shown no sign of moving out again.

'Will you mind very much if I go?' Jermaine had asked her mother—her one regret about leaving.

'It's not as if you're going to Timbuktu,' her mother had smiled—and with her blessing Jermaine had left Oxfordshire for London, and had taken residence in the small flat that Masters and Company had found for her.

Two years on, Jermaine was an established member of the sales support team. She worked with, and liaised with, the best field people in the business. Hard-working family men in the main. Sophisticated executives who had come to rely on her input, trusting her to follow up anything they initiated. She was good at her job, and loved it, and enjoyed the maturity of the men she worked with.

Three months ago she had been at a party with Stuart Evans—a man she shared an office with—when she had met Ash Tavinor. They had immediately got on well, and Jermaine hadn't been totally surprised when a few days later Ash had phoned her at her office and enquired would he be stepping on anybody's toes if he asked her out?

She'd liked him, and dined with him the very next evening. In no time she'd learned that he had just sold his apartment, more quickly than he had anticipated, and had not as yet found anything that had everything he wanted. He was still looking. In the meantime his brother had said he could move into his place and was welcome to stay as long as he liked.

'That's very good of him and his wife,' Jermaine had remarked, only to learn that Ash's brother, Lukas, was not married.

'Lukas is away more often than he's at home so we're unlikely to see each other all that often,' Ash had smiled.

A month later Ash had met her parents and—her sister. He had been totally impervious to Edwina's charms, and from then on Jermaine had allowed herself to grow fond of Ash.

But now Ash had grown weary of her backing off every time the amorous side of his nature reared its head. He wanted that commitment from her. And she—wasn't she being just a tiny bit stubborn? Hadn't Ash proved himself? He was sincere. It was her and her alone that he wanted. Wasn't she, as he'd said, being just a little bit old-fashioned? Wasn't it time she…? The phone rang. Ash!

It must be him. He had been away two whole weeks now and she had thought every day that he might think to give her a call, but he hadn't. True, he had told her he was going to be extremely busy…

She hurried to answer it. 'Hello?' she enquired brightly. It *was* Ash.

'Jermaine—um…' he began, though not cheerfully, not in his usual sunny tone. She was eager to talk to him, to ask how he'd been, how was work—she thought they knew each other well enough by now for her to ask when was she going to see him again. But—something wasn't right! Instead of sounding eager to talk to her, Ash was sounding reluctant to talk to her at all and had said nothing after that 'Jermaine—um…'

'What's wrong?' she enquired, ready to help, wanting to help if he had a problem—or so she thought *then!*

'I've—er—I've been putting off making this call,' he confessed, and sounded so much as if he would by far prefer to be talking to anybody else but her that, as shaken as she was suddenly feeling, Jermaine felt her mammoth pride spring urgently into life.

She and Ash had spent some very good times together,

but if his silence this past fortnight—no matter how busy he had been—meant he had gone off the idea of her and commitment, then she wasn't about to let him think she'd be broken-hearted if he'd rung to say that this was 'bye-bye' time.

'Let me make it easy for you,' she answered lightly. 'While I've truly enjoyed the good times we've shared, your absence this—er—past couple of weeks has shown me that, well, to be blunt, I'm not ready to make the commitment you spoke of. In actual fact,' she hurried on, pride to the fore, 'I've come to the conclusion that it would be better if we didn't see each other again.'

'Um...' Ash still seemed stuck for words. 'Actually, Jermaine, I wasn't calling to—er—um...' She waited. She still liked Ash, was still fond of him, but if he wasn't phoning to say 'It's been nice knowing you', then she hadn't the first idea what his fourteen days of silence, or his stated, 'I've been putting off making this call' was all about. 'The thing is...' he seemed to gather himself together to begin to explain '...Lukas came home unexpectedly on Saturday.'

Two days ago. 'You're phoning from home? Your brother's place?' Jermaine questioned. Ash was still looking for the right property to purchase. 'You're back from Scotland?'

There was a tense silence from the other end. Then, to her surprise, Ash confessed, 'I didn't go to Scotland.'

He'd been away two weeks but hadn't been where he had told her he was going? 'Your plans changed?' She concentrated on keeping her tone light. She still had no clue as to why Ash, if he hadn't called to say goodbye, had put off making this call. But she was more astonished than surprised when at last he answered.

'I never intended to go to Scotland,' he confessed.

'You never...? You lied to me?' The lightness had gone from her tone.

'I—couldn't help it,' Ash admitted. Jermaine's feeling of astonishment went up tenfold and, at his next three words, it mingled with a sudden familiar sickness in the pit of her stomach. 'Edwina and I...'

'Edwina?' Her voice had risen in her shock. 'Edwina, my sister?'

'We couldn't help it. We fell in love, and...'

'You've been seeing Edwina?' Jermaine couldn't take it in. 'All the time you've been ringing me, dating me, you've been...'

'It didn't start out like that,' Ash jumped in quickly.

Jermaine was reeling, but holding on—just. 'I'm sure it didn't!' Oh, weren't we on familiar territory! 'It started out with me introducing her to you at my parents' home over two months ago—have you been dating Edwina since then?' Jermaine questioned sharply.

'No!' he protested. 'And it didn't start out as a "date".' Tell me about it! 'Edwina was near my home, Highfield, Lukas's place, when she had a puncture. You must have given her my phone number because, poor darling...' *Poor darling!* I'm just loving this! '...she rang me with no idea what to do.'

Jermaine knew for a fact, since she had seen nor heard nothing from her sister this past couple of months, that by no chance had she passed on the telephone number of Highfield. 'You had, of course?'

'Yes,' Ash answered.

'You never mentioned Edwina's "puncture" to me.'

'She asked me not to.' I'll bet she did! 'She thought you might be upset that she'd bothered me. I said you wouldn't be but Edwina said she'd feel better if it was our little secret.'

How sweet! 'So you asked her out and...?'

'I didn't. We—er—that is, Edwina found a glove in her car—it was your fathers, but she didn't know that then. Not until after she'd called in at my office one day when she was passing. And, since it was close to lunch time, suggested that the least she could do after the inconvenience she'd put me to was to take me to lunch.' Hook on to my line and let me pull you in! Edwina obviously hadn't lost her touch. 'Then you couldn't see me—that weekend you went home to look after your mother when she had flu—and...'

'Thank you for *at last* having the decency to tell me!' Jermaine chopped him off. She didn't want to hear any more; she could guess the rest. 'Goodbye, Ash,' she added with quiet dignity.

'That wasn't why I phoned!' Ash cried in panic before she could put the phone down.

She hesitated. She needed time, space to lick her wounds. Edwina had done it again! 'It wasn't?'

'Edwina's had an accident!'

Fear struck her. She did not particularly like her sister—but that didn't stop her from loving her. 'What sort of an accident? Is she badly hurt? Where is she? Which hospit—?'

'She isn't in hospital. It isn't as serious as that. She's here—at Highfield.'

Highfield! 'Your brother's place? Edwina's at your brother's home?'

'We've—er—had a little holiday here,' Ash owned reluctantly. 'She intended to go back to her place yesterday, but...'

Edwina had been holidaying with Ash! A two-week holiday! Jermaine was shaken anew. She supposed she shouldn't really be shaken by anything Edwina did, so perhaps it was the fact it was Ash—her own boyfriend—correction, *ex*-boyfriend—who was her sister's holiday boyfriend that was the real shaker. All this while Jermaine had thought him too up to his ears in work in Scotland to get near a phone—and he had been holiday all the while with her sister at his brother's home in Hertfordshire!

But—Edwina was hurt in some way. 'What's wrong with her—what sort of an accident?'

'As I said, Lukas came home unexpectedly on Saturday. He's been away for about a month and was pretty shattered. So, to give him a chance to unwind a bit, I took Edwina down to the local riding stables and we hired a couple of horses. Only Edwina's mount was a bit more spirited than we were told, and galloped off with her. When I caught up with them, Edwina was lying on the ground, stunned. She'd taken a dreadful tumble and hurt her back.'

'What does the doctor say?' Jermaine asked urgently.

'Poor darling, she's so brave—she's refused point-blank to see a doctor.'

'She's refused...? Can she walk?'

'Oh, yes. But with great difficulty. Between us, Mrs Dobson and I—she's Lukas's housekeeper—' he explained, 'got Edwina upstairs and into bed. She's there now. She tried to insist on getting up, but when she fainted I made her stay exactly where she was.'

Fainted! Suspicions which she did not want began to stir in Jermaine's mind. How well she remembered how conveniently Edwina would limp with some knee injury or other should she be called upon to do some errand she wasn't keen on. Jermaine clearly recalled when she had been thirteen, Edwina seventeen, and Edwina, who had had her own small car, had been in a fury because her mother wouldn't allow her to borrow her much larger and zippier car. There had been a fearful screaming match, Jermaine remembered. It had ended with Edwina flouncing out of the drawing room. Her mother had gone after her a minute later—and had found Edwina in a dead 'faint'. Only

Jermaine, who had rushed out at her mother's call, had seen the way Edwina had surreptitiously peeped beneath her lashes to see how her 'faint' was going down. Not many weeks afterwards Edwina's car had been changed for her first sports car.

'So you see, Mrs Dobson has looked after Edwina, but now she's busy with her other duties,' Ash was going on. 'And although I know I've got a colossal neck to ask it of you, I just had to ring to ask if you'll come down to Highfield and look after your sister?'

'Colossal neck' was putting it mildly. 'I'd better have a word with her,' Jermaine answered coolly, feeling mean for her suspicions, but years of living with her sister had left few blindfolds.

'She doesn't know I'm ringing!' Ash exclaimed. 'She'd have a fit if she did. I didn't want to ring at all, which is why I'm ringing so late after her accident. But Lukas has just asked what family Edwina has and seems to think that you, as her only sister, would be sure to want to come down to Highfield to look after her, so...'

'Now wait a minute!' Go down to Highfield? Go to look after her back-stabbing, excellent horse-woman sister who, more than probably—if past knowledge of her was anything to go by—had not hurt her back as badly as she was making out? 'I've a job to go to. I can't drop everything and come dashing down to Hertfordshire just because...'

'Just because?' He sounded horrified. 'Edwina's your sister...' he began to remonstrate.

'And she's *your* girlfriend!' Guilt at the small percentage of doubt that remained, because maybe Edwina had seriously injured her back, made Jermaine's voice sharp. 'You look after her!' she told Ash, and discontinued the call.

She couldn't rest, of course. Jermaine paced her small flat, furious with Ash, angry with Edwina—but plagued by conscience. Drat, and double drat. Then she remembered the mobile phone from which Edwina was never parted. In seconds Jermaine had dialled the number.

'Hello?' enquired a sweet, totally feminine voice.

'Thanks for pinching Ash. How's your back?' Jermaine opened with sisterly candour.

'He *rang* you?' Edwina was clearly outraged, her sweet tone swiftly departing, sounding not the slightest abashed that Jermaine knew about her and Ash. 'He had no right...'

Edwina could talk of *right!* 'Why wouldn't he ring— with you "suffering" the way you are.'

'Stuff that—you should see his brother!'

Click. In that one sentence Jermaine, who knew her sister so well, had it all worked out. The wealthy elder brother, bachelor brother, had returned home unexpectedly and Edwina—never one to miss a chance and already established at Highfield—had no intention of removing herself from his orbit. Due to leave Highfield the next day, Edwina must have had her greedy little brain working furiously in her endeavour to find some way of lingering on at Highfield. Jermaine saw it all. Lukas Tavinor would be a much better catch than his brother. Poor Ash; like the proverbial hot coal, he would be dropped.

'You're a better rider than Ash?'

'He'd barely settled in his saddle when I took off,' Edwina boasted.

'He wants me to come down and "look after" you.'

'Don't you *dare!*' Edwina shrieked.

'Don't worry, I wasn't going to,' Jermaine retorted, and hung up.

Well, she had no need to feel guilty any more, Jermaine fumed. All too plainly there was nothing wrong with Edwina's back. Her 'accident' had merely been a means to an end. By the sound of it, the globe-trotting Lukas Tavinor was back in England for a short while—Edwina wanted to be 'on the spot' while he was still around, and before he went away again. And what Edwina wanted, she invariably got.

Jermaine was familiar with her sister's tactics, yet even so it still shook her that there had not been a scrap of remorse from Edwina, or apology, for 'holidaying' with her younger sister's boyfriend. Edwina had cared not a bit, nor felt any need to pretend when they'd been on the phone just now. She had not hurt her back, but took Jermaine's loyalty for granted, assuming without question that she would not tell anyone what a humbug Edwina really was.

And the devil of it was, Jermaine fumed, Edwina was right. Edwina had done nothing to earn her loyalty, but she had it. She knew Jermaine wouldn't be telling Ash what a fraud she was. But he had enough to learn. Jermaine went to bed wondering if he knew yet that he and Edwina were history.

By morning Jermaine was coming to terms with her ex-boyfriend's duplicity and was starting to feel a little incredulous that she had ever given more than a passing thought to the sort of commitment Ash had wanted. Good grief, he was as fickle as the rest of them! She had been so sure about him too. So sure that he wasn't remotely interested in Edwina.

Well, it was doubly certain now that the next man who dated Jermaine Hargreaves had better not try the 'commitment' angle. She positively was not interested. Come to that, she wasn't interested in dating again either. She had a good job; she'd concentrate on that.

Thinking of which, Jermaine left her flat and drove to her place of work, aware as ever that something seemed to cut off in her when her boyfriends strayed in her sister's direction—Jermaine was no longer attracted to them and Edwina was welcome to the spoils. One or two had come back, pleading for a second chance, but Jermaine just hadn't wanted to know.

It was the same with Ash—she had lost interest in him. She had enjoyed his company but should he ever again ask her to go out with him then she would tell him, quite truthfully, thanks, but no thanks.

And, having moved on, Ash Tavinor would become someone she once knew, and would be no more than that—Jermaine got on with her work.

'Coming for a swift half?' Stuart Evans invited when they were clearing their desks for the day.

She had nothing else pressing, and Stuart was more a friend than anything else. No way could his invitation be construed as a date. 'Since you ask,' she accepted, and the 'swift half' turned out to be a bar meal. Jermaine arrived home around nine to hear her phone ringing.

'It's Ash,' he said as soon as she answered.

Ash who? or *Hi?* Since she knew full well that there was nothing whatsoever the matter with Edwina, Jermaine simply couldn't bring herself to enquire how she was. 'How's Ash?' she enquired instead.

'Look, Jermaine, couldn't you come and look after Edwina? Not that there's a lot to do,' he added quickly. 'The poor darling's talking of going back to her place—she doesn't want to be a nuisance. But I can't let her do that and...'

'In case you didn't hear me last night—I have a job to go to.' Jermaine cut him off, with no intention at all of going down to Highfield to hold her sister's hand.

'I never knew you were so hard!' Ash complained.

Hard! 'Let me put it this way. Edwina's your holiday companion—take an extended vacation.' There was a brief silence, but if Ash was drumming up some kind of an argument, Jermaine didn't want to know. 'Goodbye, Ash,' she bade him, and had barely put the phone down before it rang again.

'Have you no concern at all about your sister?' enquired

a harsh voice she had never heard before—though her mind was working overtime as to whom her caller might be.

Jermaine only just managed to bite back a snappy retort. She swallowed hard. 'Good evening,' she managed pleasantly.

'Your place is here, looking after your sister, not staying out half the night.'

It was only a little after nine o'clock! Which monastery had he sprung from? Jermaine strove hard for control. 'Have we been introduced?' she tossed in shortly.

'Lukas Tavinor!' he barked—as she'd surmised, Ash's brother. 'Ash has an important meeting he can't miss tomorrow. You'd better come now and...'

At which point Jermaine lost the small control she had over her annoyance with the whole lot of them. '*I've* got an important meeting tomorrow!' snapped she who hadn't, not caring at all for his tone, much less his orders. 'Edwina's your guest—*you* look after her.'

A tense silence was her immediate answer. Followed by a clipped, 'Ash was wrong to suggest I should try ringing you. You *are* as hard as he said you were.'

Jermaine's breath caught. She didn't even know this man, yet here he was ready to brand her—when all she'd done was to go out with his brother. This, and his brother's duplicity, was what she received for her trouble!

'That's right,' she agreed.

'You won't...?'

'I won't.'

'My...' He seemed to find her insensitivity beyond words.

'Oh—go and play with your train set!' she erupted, and abruptly terminated his call.

Suddenly she was the bad lot in all of this! Jermaine felt like throwing something. She didn't even know the man.

He didn't know her. Yet, even so, he was ready to believe her to be heartless!

Well, on reflection she supposed it did look bad. But it wouldn't look half so bad if Lukas Tavinor knew the truth—that all time she'd believed his brother was her boy-friend he had been dallying with her sister. Not that Jermaine was likely to tell him. And it certainly didn't sound as if Ash had. But she could sit back with a feeling of relief; at least her parting remark had ended any odd chance that Lukas Tavinor Esquire might telephone her again.

Strangely, when the day before Jermaine had thought frequently of how when she had been cosily imagining Ash slaving away in Scotland he had been cosily having a fine old holiday with her sister, it seemed the following day to be his brother that occupied quite a few spare moments.

She'd got the impression that Lukas Tavinor had rather a nice voice, though there had been little to hear of it in the harsh way he had spoken to her. Who did he think he was anyway? He didn't know her. In fact, he knew nothing about her. Other, of course, than what Ash and Edwina had told him.

While Jermaine wouldn't put it past her sister to put a little poison down if it would elect some sympathy from Lukas Tavinor, Jermaine couldn't think that the three months she had gone out with Ash counted for nothing. She had always thought him to have honesty and integrity. Which, if that was true, must mean he was pretty besotted by Edwina to have been carrying on a liaison with her while still going out with her sister.

All of which meant that Ash was going to be the one to be hurt when all of this was over. For, as sure as night followed day, Edwina was going to dump him when it suited her.

It was at that moment that Jermaine, finally over her

shock at Ash's behaviour, all at once realised that she would never have made that commitment to him which he had at one time wanted. She had been fond of him, but her emotions, she now knew, had not been any deeper than that.

Jermaine went home from her office having come to terms with Ash's duplicity and realising that she still felt a little fond of him. Fond enough anyway to know that she didn't want him to feel very badly hurt when Edwina gave him the big heave-ho.

Jermaine made herself something to eat, wondering again about his brother. Lukas sounded a particularly nasty piece of work. She smiled. Wouldn't it be wonderful if Edwina pulled it off? From the little she knew of Lukas—and, thank you very much, she didn't want any more communication with him—they seemed exactly right for each other.

She was still having rosy dreams of one Edwina Hargreaves and one Lukas Tavinor giving each other hell when there was a ring at her doorbell. Thinking it might be one of her neighbours, Jermaine went to the door. But, on opening it, she saw not a neighbour but a tall, dark-haired, firm-jawed, mid-thirties man standing there.

The fact that he was immaculately suited told her he hadn't come to read the electricity meter. Add to that the grim look about him, and Jermaine's own anticipatory welcoming smile went into hiding.

He said nothing, this man, until those steady grey eyes had fully taken in her platinum-blonde hair—loose about her shoulders—her large violet eyes, and her slender yet curvaceous body.

'And you are?' She hadn't intended to say a word.

'Tavinor!' he clipped.

Her insides gave a funny little squiggle. Grief—and she'd not long since decided she didn't want anything further to do with him! 'Which one?' she snapped right back, knowing full well he had to be Lukas—surely there couldn't be three of them!

'You're already acquainted with my brother, Ash, I believe.'

Like we'd had something going from strength to strength before I introduced my sister—oh, does she have a nice surprise waiting for you, Lukas Tavinor! How fast can you run? 'We have met,' Jermaine concurred.

'Are we going to have this discussion on your doorstep?' he demanded.

It wouldn't have taken much for her to have said no and shut the door; end of discussion. But manners were manners, and, regrettably, she had a few. 'Come in,' she invited, and led the way to her small but, thanks to her mother's insistence, very pleasantly carpeted and furnished sitting room.

Jermaine knew why he'd come. She opened her mouth to tell him 'Not a chance' but he got in first. 'I thought perhaps I should call to personally appeal to you to come to Highfield to do your duty to your sister,' he said without preamble.

You don't appeal to me personally or any other way, Jermaine fumed, not taking kindly to that 'duty' dig. 'I trust you haven't come very far out of your way, for nothing,' she hinted.

'Aren't you interested in your sister's well-being?' he demanded, her hint not lost on him.

For a moment she was stumped for a reply, but, since loyalty forbade her from telling him what a fraud her sister was being, Jermaine settled for, 'I'm sure Edwina must be feeling better by now.'

'Is that all you can say?' he enquired harshly.

Jermaine had suddenly had enough of the whole of it. Ash, Edwina, and now *him*. 'Look,' she said snappily, 'if you're that concerned somebody should look after her, hire a nurse!' He'd got pots of money—he could afford it.

'I've offered to get a nurse in. Your sister wouldn't hear of robbing some other patient of a nurses' expert services.'

I'll bet she wouldn't hear of it. It wouldn't take a nurse very long to realise that there was very little the matter with Edwina's back. 'Then Edwina will have to put up with it without a nurse!' Jermaine stood her ground to tell Lukas Tavinor.

He didn't like it; he didn't like her tone. Jermaine could tell that from the slightest narrowing of his eyes. She had an idea that few opposed this man and got away with it. Oh, my word, that jaw looked tough.

'And that's your last word?' he questioned grimly.

'"Goodbye" seems a better one,' she said sweetly, and didn't miss the glint that came to his suddenly steely grey eyes the moment before she moved round him and went and opened the door wide.

Without a word he strode straight past her, and Jermaine closed the door after him and went back to her sitting room—and found that her hands were shaking.

For heaven's sake, what was the matter with her? She'd repeated to Tavinor what she'd told him on the phone last night, that she was not going to go anywhere near Highfield, his home, to look after her sister. And that was the end of it—so why did she think that, somehow, she hadn't heard the last of it?

CHAPTER TWO

MEMORY of a pair of grey eyes glinting steel made Jermaine leave her bed the next morning well before her alarm went off. Ridiculous, she fumed, as she showered and went over yet again Lukas Tavinor's visit last night. She was giving the man far too much space in her head. For goodness' sake, she hardly knew him—and no way on this earth could he make her go down to Highfield to 'look after' her sister.

Jermaine tossed him out of her head. Overbearing pig—who did he think he was? She went to work, however, with the feeling starting to creep in that she wasn't too happy that anyone should think her the unfeeling kind of monster that Tavinor, and his younger brother, obviously believed her to be. But, since she couldn't very well tell either of them what an utter sham her sister was, Jermaine knew that she was stuck with the 'unfeeling monster' label.

'Come out with me tonight and make all my dreams come true?' Tony Casbolt, ace flirt, waltzed into her office with his usual Thursday offer.

'I'm shampooing the dog,' she answered without looking up.

Tony knew as well as everyone else that she didn't have a dog; he never gave up. 'One of these days you'll say yes, and I'll be shampooing my cat,' he threatened.

She laughed. She liked him. But she wasn't laughing a half an hour later when she took a call from her mother. Her mother rarely phoned her at her office.

'Are you all right?' Jermaine asked quickly; her mother sounded rather strained.

'I think so—but your father's getting himself into a state.'

'What's the matter with him?' Jermaine questioned, ready to drop everything and dash to her parents' home.

'We've just had a visit from Ash Tavinor's brother.'

'Lukas!' Jermaine exclaimed in absolute astonishment.

'Oh, you know him?' her mother asked, but didn't wait for a reply as she went on, 'I know you went out with Ash several times; you brought him here once. But he's apparently been going out with Edwina since you stopped seeing him. Anyhow, she's been staying at the Tavinor home, and has injured her back slightly. Since Lukas was passing this way, he called in to personally tell us not to be alarmed, but that she might feel better if one of us went to see her.'

He'd been to see her parents! Jermaine couldn't believe it. The utterly unspeakable swine. Since Tavinor was *passing,* my aunt Mabel! The devious toad had made a special journey or she was a Dutchman.

'I've spoken to her on the phone, and she's fine.' Jermaine immediately put her mother's mind at rest.

'You have? But you've not seen her?'

'No,' Jermaine admitted carefully.

'I shall have to go and look after her. Your father won't rest until one of us does, and you know how hopeless he is in a sickroom.

'Mum, there's no...' 'Need' she would have said, but her mother interrupted.

'I'll have to. You know your father.'

Indeed she did. And at that point Jermaine knew, galling though it was to accept, that Tavinor, L. had won. 'I'll go,' she said, as she knew she must. Her father would go on and on until one of them had seen and reported on Edwina. He would be beside himself if anything happened to her— it would be pointless telling him that his eldest daughter hadn't hurt herself at all.

'Will you love? I'll go if...'

Jermaine wouldn't hear of it. The bout of flu her mother had suffered had been particularly exhausting and she was only now getting back to her former strength. No way was Jermaine going to have her fetching and carrying for Edwina—as she knew full well Edwina would let her.

'I'll go and see her tonight after work. How's that?'

'And you'll ring as soon as you can?'

Jermaine promised she would, and ended the call with steam very nearly coming out of her ears. How could he? How *could* he? Okay, so her parents weren't in their dotage, but Tavinor hadn't known that when he'd gone to see them.

Barely knowing what she was doing, she was so incensed, Jermaine grabbed the phone and dialled the number she had occasionally dialled when she'd needed to delay meeting Ash when work had taken precedence.

'International Systems,' answered a voice she remembered.

'It's not Ash I want this time—' Jermaine put a smile in her voice '—but Lukas Tavinor. Is he in?' Too late Jermaine realised what, in her fury, she had overlooked. If her parents had only just had a visit from Lukas Tavinor, then he couldn't yet be back at his office.

'I'm afraid he's not answering, and his PA is off sick. Is it personal, or can anyone else...?'

'May I leave a message for him to ring me? Jermaine Hargreaves.' She gave her name, and also where she might be reached.

She was still angry when she went out for some air at lunchtime. Seeing the brightly lit shops all festive with Christmas decorations did nothing to calm her sense of outrage. In fact the more she thought of what Tavinor had done, the more furious she became. Suddenly a date with

Tony Casbolt that night seemed a better idea than what she was committed to do.

She was still kicking against what she had to do when Stuart left the office, saying he'd be away about fifteen minutes. Only seconds later her loathing of what she had to do peaked, and she quickly dialled her sister's mobile phone.

Unbelievably, Edwina wasn't answering. Jermaine let go an exasperated sigh. So much for her notion to get Edwina to phone their parents to tell them she was fine. Not that there was any guarantee that Edwina *would* phone, even if she said she would.

Hating that Lukas Tavinor should dominate not only her thoughts but her actions as well—no *way* did she want to make that journey tonight—Jermaine rang his home. Ash answered. She put the phone down without speaking. What was the point?

It was just after four when the phone on her desk rang. Jermaine was glad that she again had the office to herself— her caller was Lukas Tavinor.

She did not thank him for returning her call, but in less than a second went from standing still into furious orbit. 'How *dare* you descend on my parents?' she blazed. 'How *dare*...'

'You have my address?' Obviously a very busy man, he chopped her off mid-rant, and Jermaine hated him with a vengeance. This arrogant pig of a man, this overbearing, odious rat, was totally confident she would be going to his home that night. She was too choked with rage to speak. 'Or perhaps you'd prefer me to call for you on my way home,' he suggested smoothly.

Jermaine took a deep and semi-controlling breath. 'I'll make my own way!' she snapped. 'Where do you live?'

She hated him afresh, because there was a smile in his voice as he gave her directions. And she wasn't sure, had he been near, that she wouldn't have hit him, when, silkily, he added, 'Don't forget your nightie and a toothbrush.'

Jermaine slammed the phone down. What a skunk! She wasn't staying that long. A quick look at Edwina so she could truthfully tell her parents that Edwina had 'fully recovered', then she would be back in her car and on her way. She would be sleeping in her own bed that night.

Events, however, transpired against her. She was ten minutes away from leaving her desk to go home to grab a quick bite to eat—no way was she going to dine at *that* man's table—when Chris Kepple, one of her favourite executives, phoned in asking her if she could get a quote and some brochures out that night.

'I'm sorry to drop it on you this late, but I've been with my client all day and I wouldn't like him to feel our efficiency is any less brilliant than he's sure it is. You can scold me the next time you see me,' he promised.

Jermaine laughed. 'I'll hold you to that,' she answered, and took down the details of his day's business and got on with it. She eventually finished her day's work at seven-thirty, and was halfway to her flat before she unwound sufficiently from that last couple of hectic hours to consider she might have done better to have driven straight to Hertfordshire. It was a foul night—wind, rain, storm and tempest—and she could have been part way there by now.

Rain lashed the windows as she stood in her kitchen eating a hasty sandwich and drinking a quick cup of coffee. She still had not the smallest intention of staying overnight at Highfield but, just in case she hadn't found the place by midnight and had to put up at some hotel, she tossed a few things in an overnight bag and went out to her car.

The rain had lessened as Jermaine headed her car in the direction of Hertfordshire. She drove along reflecting that, for the sake of her parents' peace of mind, she was going to have to fulfil this wild goose chase—and realising that no matter how late she got there she would have to telephone them; they were waiting for her call.

Rain began again before she was anywhere near to Highfield. Deluging down thick and fast, too fast for it to drain quickly away from the country roads on which she was travelling. The result being that she had to check her speed and cautiously make her way.

She mutinied against her sister, she mutinied against Ash Tavinor, but most of all she mutinied against Lukas Tavinor, who that day had had the unmitigated effrontery to go and see her parents.

By the time Jermaine eventually came to Highfield she was not very taken with any of its inhabitants. This was ridiculous, totally ridiculous. There was nothing in the world the matter with Edwina. Nothing at all. It was only because of wretched sisterly loyalty, Jermaine fumed, that she had been unable to tell anybody about it. That Edwina did not feel the same loyalty to her, or she would never have made a play for Ash, didn't seem to alter anything. Jermaine sighed. Stupid though she knew it was, she couldn't help remaining loyal to Edwina.

Highfield, as its name suggested, was built on highish ground, and as Jermaine steered her way she was glad to find there were no more stretches of water to negotiate around; all water was running downhill.

Her feeling of mutiny against the house's occupants dipped slightly when she noticed that someone had left the porch lights on, as if to guide her. She studied the stone façade of the elegant old building; she found it truly quite lovely.

But this would never do. Giving herself a mental shake, Jermaine left her car and sprinted for cover from the torrential downpour. Under the cover of the stone-pillared porch, she rang the doorbell. She was not kept waiting very long.

Lukas Tavinor himself pulled back the stout front door and for several seconds just stood looking at her. But Jermaine had had enough of this. He might be tall, he might be dark, he might be good-looking, but rain was pelting in at her and she did not want to be here anyway.

'You want a discussion on *your* doorstep?' she questioned disagreeably, and disliked him some more when she actually thought she saw his lips twitch. If he was laughing at her she'd...

'Where's your case?' he asked.

Jermaine, confused that he might be laughing at her, angry at him and this whole wretched business, and having fallen instantly in love with his house, found she was telling him, 'It's in my car.'

In the next second she had got herself into more of one piece, but by then he was ushering over his threshold while telling her, 'I'll get it later. Come in out of this rain.'

The inside lived up to the outside, all lush warm wood panelling hung with various oil paintings. But as she stood there while Tavinor closed the door Jermaine reminded herself that she wasn't here on any pleasure trip, and her case, in this instance her overnight bag, was staying exactly where it was—in her car.

'Where's Edwina?' Jermaine questioned promptly. Get this over with and she was out of here.

'In the drawing room.'

She'd managed to drag herself out of bed, then? Though, of course, since Lukas Tavinor and his bank balance were what Edwina cared about, she'd hardly be likely to ensnare him while hiding herself away in bed.

'You've told Edwina I was coming?' Jermaine asked as he escorted her along the hall.

She was looking at him as he glanced to her and shook his head. 'I thought we'd give her a nice surprise,' he answered blandly, so blandly that for a fleeting moment

Jermaine had an uncanny kind of feeling that this clever man staring down at her so mildly had seen through Edwina. Had seen through her and was on to all her wiles.

Oh, heavens! Though before she could blush from the embarrassment of thinking that Edwina was making a fool of herself, Jermaine countered any such idea. Men fell for Edwina like ninepins. Lukas Tavinor might be clever in business, but he was a man, wasn't he? Besides which there was nothing in his expression now to so much as hint that he knew Edwina was playing to the gallery.

Then he was opening the drawing room door. How cosy! There was Edwina, feet up on the sofa. There was Ash... Though, come to think of it, Jermaine had seen him looking happier.

'Jermaine!'

It was not her sister who exclaimed her name but Ash, as he beamed a smile at her and hurried over. 'You came!' he cried, and appeared so pleased to see her he bent as if to kiss her.

Jermaine gave him a frosty look for his trouble, but as she pulled back of out his reach she caught his elder brother speculatively observing them. She met Lukas's gaze full-on, and let him have a helping of frost too.

She wanted out of there! None of these people were doing her blood pressure the slightest good. One way and another she seemed to have been in a permanent state of anger ever since Ash's phone call three days ago. Since his brother had joined in the act, two days ago, she had gone from mere vexation to a constant state of uproar!

Jermaine decided to ignore both men and approached the sofa where her sister was so prettily draped. Edwina was too good an actress to show her displeasure while the others were in the room, but Jermaine knew her well enough not to miss the hostility in her 'What are you doing here?'

'How are you feeling?' Jermaine asked, hating the role

she was forced to play—but it was that or show her sister up as the fraud she was.

'Oh, I'm much, much better.' Edwina smiled fragilely.

'Edwina's been so brave.' Ash joined them to look down at his new love.

There didn't seem much of an answer to that, Jermaine fumed. But she'd already had enough of perjuring her soul by asking Edwina how she was. Jermaine turned and saw that Lukas Tavinor was still silently observing the tableau. Though, since his expression was inscrutable, what he was thinking was anybody's guess.

'May I use your phone?' she asked, tilting her chin a proud fraction. It was humiliating having to come here and start play-acting—but it was all his fault. If he hadn't deliberately gone to see her parents...

'There's a phone in the hall,' he replied evenly, and went with her from the drawing room and out into the hall. Though his tone had toughened, she noticed, when, as she looked about the wide and splendid hall for a phone, he abruptly challenged, 'Won't the boyfriend wait?'

Get him! 'For ever, if need be,' she answered snootily—like she was going to tell him she'd been dumped by her boyfriend, his brother, in favour of her sister.

'You've only just got here—did you promise to ring him as soon as you'd landed?'

Jermaine stared at him, her lovely violet eyes going wide. What *was* this? 'Thanks to you, and your colossal cheek in alarming my parents, I need to ring them to tell them that Edwina isn't as badly hurt as you must have made out to them,' she hissed.

He smiled. She hated him. 'Perhaps you'd like to make your call in the privacy of my study?' he offered, and was leading the way before she could hit him.

She hadn't seen him smile before, though. And, while she was still angry with him, she had to admit there was something fairly shattering about him when he smiled. His smile seemed infectious, somehow. Not that she was going to smile back—perish the thought.

Nor was she smiling a minute later when—so much for privacy—he closed his study door—but with him on the inside. 'Thank you,' Jermaine said nicely. He didn't budge. She looked pointedly at the door—he seemed to find his turned-off computer of interest. Jermaine turned her back on him, picked up the phone and dialled. Her father answered straight away. 'Edwina's fine,' she told him, knowing that that was what he wanted to hear in preference to anything else.

'You've seen her?'

'I'm with her now.'

'Can't she come to the phone herself?'

'Well, I'm not actually in the same room,' Jermaine explained. 'I'm at Highfield, Ash's place.' She was aware of the elder Tavinor breathing down her neck and, though when she never, ever got flustered, she started feeling all edgy inside. 'Well, it's his brother Lukas's place, actually,' she corrected.

'That would be the man who came to see us this morning?'

'He shouldn't have,' she rallied. If he was staying to hear her private conversation, he could hear this as well. 'He had no right at all to call and to worry you so. He...'

'He had every right, Jermaine,' her father retorted sharply. 'I've since spoken to Ash, and he tells me *you* knew on *Monday* that your sister was injured. You should have told me straight away!'

'But...'

'It was you who had no *right* not to tell us. Your mother said you'd spoken to Edwina, but I thought it was only today you'd spoken to her. Ash Tavinor told me you've known she was injured since Monday.'

Jermaine was not very happy at being taken to task by her father, and, had not Lukas Tavinor been listening to her every word, she wasn't sure she wouldn't have told her father that his dear Edwina was only pretending to have hurt her back for her own ends. He'd be furious with his younger daughter, of course, but, while he had never been able to see any wrong in Edwina, surely he couldn't be so completely blinkered to some of his eldest daughter's less loveable traits?

But Lukas Tavinor *was* listening and all Jermaine could think of to say to her father was, 'I'm sorry.'

'So you should be. Ash wants you to stay with Edwina—just mind that you do.'

Jermaine sighed. She was used to coming second where her father and Edwina were concerned. 'I'll get Edwina to ring you tomorrow,' she promised.

'Not if it's going to cause her pain to come to the phone. You can ring me to tell me what sort of a night she's had.'

'Give my love to Mum,' Jermaine said quietly and put the phone down ready to strangle her sister—and not feeling too well disposed to the man who strolled into her line of vision either. 'I hate you,' she snapped, tossing him a belligerent look.

'That makes a change,' he replied urbanely. 'Women are usually falling at my feet.' Jermaine added seething dislike to her look. He grinned. 'Did your father give you hell?'

'Thanks to you.'

'You should have come when you were called,' Lukas replied, totally unabashed.

'I came, I saw,' she answered shortly, 'and I'm going home.'

'Oh, your father wouldn't like that,' Lukas mocked.

'You'd tell him?' she questioned, staring at him in disbelief.

'You bet I would.'

What a swine the man was. 'Why?' she asked angrily.

'Why?' He shrugged. 'Because Mrs Dobson, my treasure of a housekeeper, is getting on in years, that's why. Because she gets upset at the thought of retiring and wants to keep on working, I wouldn't dream of letting her go. That doesn't mean I want her running upstairs ten times a day to attend to your sister when that job is so obviously yours—that's why!'

Jermaine came close then to telling him that there was nothing wrong with her sister. But he wouldn't believe her anyhow, would again think her hard and unfeeling and prepared to blacken her injured sister's name rather than stay and do her sisterly duty. Jermaine felt then that she had taken enough. But, having come near to denouncing her sister and letting them all go to the devil, she discovered that family loyalty was still stronger than her own fed-up feelings. Because she couldn't do it. Instead, her tone firm and unequivocal, she told him bluntly, 'I'll stay tonight. But I'm going to work—at my office—in the morning.'

Grey eyes stared hard into her wide violet eyes. Then he smiled, a gentle smile, and her insides acted most peculiarly. 'Allow me to show you to your room,' he suggested quietly.

That gentle smile, his quiet manner, seemed to have the strangest effect on her. Because, instead of mutinying some more that her plans appeared to be getting away from her, Jermaine found she was standing meekly by while he went out into the foulness of that stormy night and collected her overnight bag from her car.

Unprotesting, she went up the wide wooden staircase with him, turning right and going along the landing with him to a room at the far end. He opened the door to a beautifully furnished room with not a speck of dust to be seen, the double bed already made up. Jermaine did protest then.

'I shouldn't have come.'

'I asked you to come. Pressed you to come,' Lukas reminded her.

'All I've done is given your Mrs Dobson more work.'

'My Mrs Dobson has help during the week,' he answered, a teasing kind of note in his voice, his grey eyes fixed on Jermaine's regretful look. 'Sharon probably "did and dusted". Now, you get settled here and I'll get you something to eat.'

That surprised her. '*You* will?'

'Knowing you were on your way to look after your sister, I have given Mrs Dobson the night off. What kept you, incidentally?'

'I worked late,' Jermaine replied—before it abruptly came to her that she was being far too friendly with someone who had more or less coerced her to come to his home that night—a man she had not so very long ago declared she hated. 'And I've already eaten,' she added snappily, 'so you can leave your chef's hat on its peg!'

His eyes narrowed at her tone, and he took a step towards the door. 'And there was me trying to be pleasant,' he commented, and she guessed he had more from instinct than desire accidentally fallen into the role of host—ensuring that his guest wanted for nothing.

'You don't have to bother on my account,' she retorted. And just in case he thought she might be joining them downstairs once she had 'settled', 'I'm going to bed!' she announced firmly. 'I need to be up early in the morning.'

'Presumably you intend to help your sister comfortably into bed before you put your lights out. That, after all, is why you're here.'

Jermaine glared at him. Ooh, how she hated him. She was here because she had no option. She did not thank him that he had just reminded her that, but for her being there to do her family duty, he wouldn't have given her house room.

She sent him a seething look of dislike, which speared him not at all, and he favoured her with a steely grey-eyed look and went from her room.

Men! She hated the lot of them. Well, perhaps that was a bit sweeping. She liked the men she worked with, and her father most of the time. But the Tavinor brothers—pfff!

Because she knew she was going to go and have a few words with her sister at whatever time the 'invalid' decided she must return to her room, Jermaine unpacked her bag, showered and donned her nightdress and the lightweight robe she had thought to throw in. A very short while later she heard sounds that indicated that Edwina was being 'assisted' up the stairs.

Some minutes later Jermaine was wishing she had thought to ask Tavinor which room was her sister's. She didn't fancy going along the landing trying all doors until she came to the right one—though she wouldn't mind waking up Tavinor if he was already fast asleep.

Then someone came and knocked at her door. She discounted that it might be Edwina—she'd be 'struggling' to walk at all. Jermaine went and opened her door, and as Lukas Tavinor stared down at her, his eyes going over her face, completely free of make-up, so she felt stumped to say a word.

He seemed pretty much the same, she thought, then immediately cancelled any such notion. Because, although that gentle look was there about him again, he wasn't at all stuck for words. However, what he had to say was the last thing she would have expected him to say.

For softly it was that he murmured, 'You know, Jermaine, you're incredibly beautiful.'

Her heart gave a jerky beat and she wasn't sure her mouth didn't fall open. She firmed her lips anyway, when she saw his glance go to her mouth, and from somewhere she gained some strength to tell him acidly, 'I'm still not falling at your feet!'

He was amused; she could see it in his eyes, in the pleasant curve of his mouth. He didn't laugh, but stared at her for a moment longer before, 'Damn!' he mocked. 'In that case—your sister's in the room three doors down. The first one at the top of the landing.'

Which, Jermaine realised as he turned and went back the way he had come, was what he had come to let her know. Clearly he didn't fancy his sleep being disturbed if she tried his room when she decided to go looking for her sister.

Jermaine found Edwina's room without any trouble. Her light tap on the door before she went in ensured that Edwina was sitting down looking suitably helpless when Jermaine had the door open. By the time she'd closed the door after her, however, Edwina was angrily on her feet, her glance on Jermaine's night attire having made it plain she was staying the night.

'It didn't take you long to get established,' she snorted.

'I didn't expect you to be thrilled.'

'Why did you have to come at all?' Edwina demanded hostilely.

'You think I wanted to? Lukas went to see Mum and Dad this morning. He…'

'Did he now?' Edwina was soon smiling. 'He must be worried about me to do that. Perhaps he's falling in love with me.'

Jermaine was side-tracked. 'What makes you say that? Has he…?'

'There are signs,' Edwina purred. 'Little looks here and there. Small indications.'

Jermaine didn't want this conversation after all. 'What about Ash? I thought he was your ''man of the moment''.'

'You can have him back any time you want him.'
Edwina shrugged. 'I'm no longer fishing for tiddlers.'

Thanks for nothing! 'How does Ash feel about this?'

'Good Lord, I haven't told him—and don't you, either,'
she warned. 'Naturally, being in so much pain, I at once
made sure I had my own room. Ash moved my stuff out
of his, like the gent he is, and Lukas will probably never
know that Ash and I were *that* close.'

She really was a heartless madam, Jermaine fumed. She
might have been in love with Ash, for all Edwina knew,
but did that stop her from letting her know that she and
Ash had been bedroom lovers? Did it blazes! Jermaine
knew then that she would be wasting her time remonstrat-
ing with her.

'Mum and Dad are very worried about you,' she said
instead. 'I told Dad you'd ring him tomorrow.'

'The batteries are flat on my mobile. I didn't think to
bring my charger.'

'I'm sure somebody will carry you to a phone if you ask
nicely,' Jermaine suggested, knowing from experience that
Edwina would ring if she felt like it, but if she didn't she
wouldn't bother.

Edwina obviously didn't take kindly to Jermaine's manner. 'And I'm sure you've stayed long enough to have
helped me into bed half a dozen times,' she hinted nastily.

Jermaine looked at her lovely blonde-haired, blue-eyed
sister, and suddenly no longer felt it would be justice if
Edwina managed to ensnare Lukas Tavinor. Somehow, just
then, Jermaine felt that he deserved better.

CHAPTER THREE

IT WAS still dark when Jermaine awoke the next day. She lay there for a while, recollecting where she was. For someone who had never intended to stay the night, she realised, she had slept very well.

She knew she should get up and start her day—but not just yet. Strangely, where spending a night at Highfield had never been in her plans, now she somehow felt most at home here.

Which was absurd, she decided, pushing back the covers and reaching for the lamp switch. Light flooded the superb room. Work, she decided firmly. She had a long way to go, and she wanted to get Edwina's breakfast and take it up to her. Correction. She didn't want to do anything of the sort. But if she didn't get Edwina's breakfast Mrs Dobson would be expected to do it.

Dawn had not broken when she showered and dressed. Since she could not hear noises of other occupants astir, Jermaine lingered in her room, stripping her bed and putting her belongings into her overnight bag. When one last check of her room showed there was nothing else she could do to save Mrs Dobson more work, Jermaine silently left her room.

A light burning in the hall indicated that either someone was up or that the light had been left on overnight. Someone *was* up, Jermaine realised when she went to the main door and found it was already unbolted.

She saw neither hide nor hair of anyone, though, when she took her overnight bag out to her car and triggered off the outside security lights.

She didn't get to stow her bag, however, because, looking about this idyllic spot, she found her attention drawn to the elegant lamps which stood on stone posts way down the long, long drive. They had been switched on, but it was not the grounds of Highfield that particularly interested her just then—but what lay beyond. It—couldn't be? Light reflecting on—water?

Staring incredulously, Jermaine set off down the drive. She did not want to believe what her eyes were telling her, but the nearer she got to the end of the drive so she had to believe it. The road beyond was flooded!

With dawn starting to break, but determined not to trust the evidence of her eyes, she skirted the rain-sodden gardens—only to find yet more water. Unbelievably, they were *cut off!* No way was she going to be able to drive through that lot—she'd be waterlogged long before she came to any main road.

Still staggered, and unwilling to admit defeat—she had a job to go to, for goodness' sake—Jermaine trudged on. She was going to go to work. She was, she *was!* Though, as she surveyed the scene, she owned that she didn't very much fancy being stranded in the middle of a moat, should her car go so far, decide it wasn't amphibious and pack up on her.

Jermaine was some way from the house, and had skirted round the rear of the building and its outbuildings, when she came unexpectedly to a little footbridge. She went over to it and stared down at the torrent of water that was splashing about in the small stream below. Then she spotted a nearby bench and went over to it. Strangely, then, as she sat down to collect her thoughts, a feeling akin to peace started to wash over her. Should that torrent ever steady down to a ripple this would be a most tranquil spot. Even now the scene—grassy banks, the bridge, even the water—had great charm.

She guessed it hadn't rained for a couple of hours now; the bench she was seated upon was wind dried. Yet, oddly, the lighter it got and the longer she stayed there—while she was still extremely anxious to leave Highfield this morning—Jermaine discovered she began to feel less anxious than she had.

It was this place, this spot, she realised, having, without being aware of it, started to take in her surroundings. It was winter now, of course, but even when damp and flooded, and with half of the trees having shed their leaves, there was something exquisite, serene, about the spot, about the willow tree bending over the stream, the dear little wooden bridge, the silence, the peace and quiet, the...

'You're up and about early,' remarked a voice, well modulated and, strangely, not disturbing the scene.

Jermaine looked up. 'It's lovely here,' she answered Lukas Tavinor, quite without thinking.

'You find this corner a bit special?' he enquired, coming to share her bench.

'Isn't it, though?' she replied. 'So serene. You could just sit here and forget all your troubles...' She broke off, astounded—wasn't that exactly what she had just been doing? She didn't even like Lukas Tavinor, yet here she was having a friendly conversation with him! She swiftly remedied that. 'How are you going to get to work today?' she demanded.

Her change of tone was not lost on him. 'I'm not,' he replied evenly.

'You're taking the day off?'

'I doubt I'll sit at home and do nothing.'

Lucky him! He'd got a study. 'How long before this floodwater clears?' she asked grumpily, with ideas of perhaps being able to drive out around mid-morning.

'Difficult to say. If it doesn't rain again before Monday...'

'Monday!' she gasped, and had her attention drawn to her feet when, ignoring her exclamation, it appeared Tavinor had been studying them.

'While I have to say I doubt I've ever seen a prettier pair of ankles, those shoes are never going to be the same again,' he remarked.

Jermaine stared at her neat two-and-a-half-inch-heeled shoes. They were black, but since they were now caked in mud they could have been any colour.

'I've got better things to do than sit here all day,' she abruptly decided, and was on her feet and marching away from him.

He did not fall into step with her, and she told herself she was thankful for that. No doubt he'd been out and about checking for any damage to his property from the storm. Pretty ankles indeed! Was that the sort of nonsense he used on her sister? Was that the kind of thing that made Edwina think he was falling for her? Jermaine thought not. Edwina knew men and...

Edwina! Oh, grief. Monday! She could be stranded here until Monday! Play-acting—going along with this ridiculous farce because Edwina was after Lukas Tavinor! Going along with it for the next *three* days!

It was farcical. She wouldn't... Loyalty, family loyalty tripped her up. Even while Jermaine fumed against it and made herself remember how, from childhood onwards, Edwina had always taken anything that was hers, be it a toy, a game, a boyfriend, she still felt this nonsensical family loyalty to her, and knew that no matter how much she kicked against it she wouldn't give Edwina away.

Feeling thoroughly out of sorts, and this morning revising her last night's opinion and deciding that Lukas Tavinor did deserve a fate going by the name of Edwina, Jermaine slipped off her shoes and re-entered the house.

By instinct she found the kitchen, and Mrs Dobson. 'I'm

Jermaine Hargreaves,' she introduced herself to the plump, sixty-something housekeeper. 'Am I going to be very much in your way if I clean my shoes at your sink?'

'I'll do them for you...'

Jermaine wouldn't hear of it, and for the next half an hour stayed in the kitchen chatting with Mrs Dobson, when that lady wasn't popping in and out to the breakfast room. And, since Jermaine had told Tavinor that she had better things to do, yet wasn't able to get to her place of work, she assured the housekeeper that she was there to help.

Jermaine had a bit of breakfast with the housekeeper, and, having got on famously with her, insisted on preparing Edwina's breakfast. Another half an hour later and Jermaine was carrying a tray up the stairs.

She was nearing the top when a door opened on the opposite side of the landing from where she and Edwina had their rooms, and Jermaine saw Lukas appear from what she presumed was his room.

They met at the top of the stairs. 'Looking after your sister, I see,' he remarked with a glance to the tray she was carrying. Jermaine wasn't sure, had not her hands been full, that she wouldn't have thumbed her nose at him—she was certain she'd heard a mocking sort of note in his voice. As it was, all she could do was walk past him without a word.

Edwina was still in bed, but wasn't pleased to see her. 'I didn't expect you to still be here!' she exclaimed nastily.

That makes two of us. 'It's either me or a nurse, apparently,' Jermaine answered, unable to resist seeing the whites of her sister's eyes.

'Heaven forbid!' Edwina roused herself.

Jermaine took the tray over to her. 'How long do you intend to keep up this pretence?' she asked forthrightly.

'What's it to you?' Edwina asked disagreeably, her sneering tone flicking Jermaine on the raw and causing her to say more than she would have.

'Since you ask—and aside from the fact that you've got both your parents, your father in particular, in a state worrying about you, not to mention that you're disrupting the whole household here, expecting to be waited on—were it not for your injury, I would be at work today, earning my living. And talking of earning a living,' Jermaine flared, 'it wouldn't hurt you to get off your back and find yourself a job.'

'Work! Me!' Edwina exclaimed as if she'd been shot. 'I wasn't brought up to work!' That was true, Jermaine had to agree. Their father had indulged Edwina past spoiling. 'Dad wouldn't want me to soil my hands…'

'But you must know he can no longer afford to be as generous to you now as he was in the past.'

'He doesn't have to be, not for much longer,' Edwina purred, and Jermaine knew then, if she hadn't known already, that Edwina would latch on to any man who had money. In this case, Lukas Tavinor. Wasn't that the sole reason Edwina was still at Highfield? 'I'll say goodbye now,' Edwina went on as Jermaine, again for some unknown reason not thrilled that Lukas might be ensnared, went to the door. 'Just phone Lukas at his office and tell him that I became so distressed at taking you away from your boring old job that I insisted you leave at once.'

When life dealt you the occasional sticky end there were sometimes other rewards, Jermaine found, and she smiled at her sister. 'I'd love to do that, Edwina, believe me I would. But if you take a look out of your window you'll see there's water, water everywhere…'

'Water?'

'The rain came; the roads are flooded. With luck—' Jermaine smiled '—I may be able to leave on Monday.'

'*Monday!*' Edwina shrieked. Jermaine left her. She was still smiling. It was nice to score one once in a while.

She bumped into Ash as she was going along the hall to

the kitchen. 'Jermaine.' He waylaid her. She stopped and looked at him. 'You're still speaking to me?' he asked, and looked so vulnerable that she realised she was still fond of him—yet, oddly, in a different sort of way. Suddenly he seemed more a friend than a boyfriend.

'Of course,' she assured him.

'I—cheated on you,' he said. 'And—I'm sorry I hurt you—I just couldn't seem to help myself.'

Jermaine had wondered how she would feel on seeing him again, but all that was there was the same sort of affection that she had for Stuart in her office. As always happened, Ash's predilection for Edwina had killed instantly any warmer romantic feelings Jermaine might have had for him. Edwina had again cast her net and, as far as Jermaine was concerned, Edwina was welcome to him. But Edwina would very shortly be giving him her sad regrets—and Jermaine just felt sorry for him.

'We were never going to be serious, Ash,' she told him quietly.

'We weren't?' He looked surprised.

'We weren't,' she confirmed.

Ash looked a tinge put out, but that was male pride, she rather supposed. So she smiled at him, and he smiled back, and they went to go their separate ways.

'It's flooded up to the bridge,' she heard Ash say, and turned to see that Lukas was standing in his study doorway, that his brother had made the comment in passing. How long Lukas had been standing there watching her and Ash in conversation was anybody's guess.

As Ash went on his way so Jermaine strolled back to the man standing at the study door. 'I need to make another phone call,' she told him bluntly.

Without a word he stepped aside so she should enter his study. She did not expect him to vacate it this time, so wasn't disappointed when he followed her in. She took up the phone and dialled her office number.

'Mr Bateman, please, Becky,' she asked the girl on the switchboard, and glanced at Lukas while she was holding.

'You seem very pally with my brother?' he remarked.

'Perhaps he inherited *all* the Tavinor charm,' she replied sweetly, and turned her back on him when she heard the voice of her immediate boss coming down the wires. 'Matthew. It's Jermaine. I'm sorry, I won't be able to get in today. I...'

'You're not ill?'

'No, I'm fine,' she assured him. 'The thing is, I stayed the night with a relative in Hertfordshire and I can't travel in this morning.'

'Floods?' he enquired. 'That was some storm last night.'

'I'm sorry,' she apologised again, knowing how busy they always were at the office on a Friday.

'That's all right, sweet love,' Matthew answered good-humouredly. 'I'll let you work late on Monday.'

Jermaine laughed and rang off, and still had a smile on her face as she turned about. She caught Lukas's glance on her, on her laughing mouth—he seemed to enjoy seeing her happy. On reflection, she supposed that for the most part he had only ever seen the grumpy side of her.

'Thanks,' she tossed at him, and got out of there to go and see what assistance she could be to Mrs Dobson. Poor woman! Prior to Ash moving in temporarily the house-keeper had only had to cater and take care of the household for just Lukas—and from what Ash said Lukas wasn't there half his time. And now not only did she have Ash to cater for, but two other guests as well.

But, with the house running smoothly, there was only so much that the housekeeper would allow her to do, and Jermaine went to the drawing room. The house was silent, no one about. She went and looked out of the window—it was raining again, pouring down. There seemed scant hope of leaving today. But she was definitely going to work on Monday, Jermaine determined, even if she had to swim it.

She mooched about; there was no sign of Ash, and Edwina would still be languishing in bed. Jermaine thought of all the work waiting to be done at her office. Work she enjoyed doing. She owned that she needed something to do.

She went back to the kitchen; Mrs Dobson wasn't there. There were many doors along the hall. Jermaine knew the drawing room, and she knew the study. She didn't want to pry. Oh, hang it, she was a sort of guest here—albeit reluctantly, albeit unwanted. She went and knocked at the study door, and went in.

Lukas was seated at his large desk, a sheaf of papers before him. He put down his pen and leaned back in his chair, waiting for her to state her business. Even before he'd said anything, she didn't care for his attitude. 'Where do you keep your bookshelves?' she asked belligerently, adding—as her normal good manners gave her a prod—'Please.'

Lukas stared at her for a few moments. Then mockingly taunted, 'I do believe the lady's bored.'

'I'm used to being busy,' Jermaine informed him stonily. 'Mrs Dobson's run out of jobs to give me—and it's tipping it down outside so I can't go for a walk.'

Again he stared at her, studying her. 'Any good at typing reports?'

'Brilliant,' she answered, hating that she had felt the need to explain anything to him.

'You wouldn't care to type something for me, I suppose?'

It was enough that she was incarcerated here, without having to work for the wretched man. 'You suppose correctly. I wouldn't,' she replied. 'I'd rather read a book.'

He shrugged, a 'suit yourself' kind of shrug, but got up to escort her to the library. Without another word he left her there, and that was when Jermaine started feeling the meanest thing on two legs.

She had no reason to feel mean, she tried to console her conscience. She didn't want to be here. If *he* hadn't had the audacity to call on her parents, she would never have come here.

With her conscience prodding away at her, however, Jermaine found the strength of her anger against Lukas Tavinor weakening. She discovered too that she seemed unable to concentrate on searching for a book to occupy her. She didn't want to be here—she wanted to be at work.

Conscience bit again as she realised that Tavinor probably didn't want to be here either. He worked hard, and must want to be at his London office. But, in the event of not being able to get there, he couldn't even have his house to himself.

Jermaine strove desperately to keep her mutiny going. She wasn't going to type his mouldy old report; she wasn't, she wasn't. His PA could do it on Monday, when... Ah, but his PA was away from work sick.

Jermaine abandoned all pretence of looking for something to read. Wouldn't she be doing his PA as much a favour as him? His PA would have other work to catch up on when she returned to work, of that Jermaine felt sure. Really, when she thought about it, to type that report was hardly a favour to anyone. Both she and Edwina were under his roof, enjoying his hospitality. True, in her own case it was hospitality she would prefer not to have to endure, but she had no wish to be beholden to anyone, and certainly not him. To type that wretched report would perhaps go some way to repaying him a little.

The matter was settled. Before she could change her mind, and not giving herself chance to think further lest she sailed on straight past the study, Jermaine went briskly from the library. She was so against doing what her conscience dictated, though, that she didn't this time even pause to knock, but went marching into the study.

She stopped dead. Tavinor looked up—he was on the telephone to some female named Beverley. Had she followed her instinct, Jermaine would have promptly turned about and got out of there. She was sure she wasn't remotely concerned at hearing him making arrangements to meet Beverley at some art gallery in a week's time—Edwina would be thrilled. But Jermaine knew then that if she turned about and left Tavinor's study she would never enter it again. Besides, *he'd* stayed around while she'd made two telephone calls. What was sauce for the goose...

He put the phone down—too busy to stay chatting to Beverley all day, obviously, Jermaine mused sourly, hardly knowing why she felt so anti-Beverley. She didn't even know the woman!

Lukas Tavinor sat silently watching and waiting, and the moment passed when Jermaine would have told him not to curtail his love-phone calls on her account. 'So where's the computer?' she snapped instead.

Again she experienced previously unknown pugilistic tendencies when his lips twitched. 'I've an idea, deep down, you're rather a nice person,' he mocked.

It was touch and go then that Jermaine didn't turn about and march straight out of there. 'I wouldn't bank on it!' she retorted, and—when he got to his feet and moved the computer to a workstation for her—she stayed.

She had told him she was brilliant at typing reports; too late now to wish she'd been a bit more modest. For the first ten minutes she concentrated hard on being as brilliant as she had said she was. Then she became absorbed in the report she was working on, and as her fingers flew over the keyboard she could not help but admire the subject matter and the conciseness of its author.

'I think you should take a break now.' Lukas Tavinor's voice cut into her absorption with the work in hand.

Jermaine looked up. 'What?'

'Mrs Dobson will have some sort of a meal ready for us.'

Jermaine got herself together. 'You're good,' she said begrudgingly, and started to print what she had so far typed.

'Not brilliant?'

Was he teasing? Looking up at him, she stared into serious grey eyes. For the moment that steely glint was missing, but she thought she saw a gleam of something else—humour, perhaps. Her heart gave a crazy little flutter—which she at once denied and went to check the first of the printing.

But Lukas was there before her. Their hands touched as they both reached for the same piece of paper. She pulled back quickly, realising this whole nightmare was having more effect on her than she'd thought—she had felt tingly all over for a moment or two then.

She watched as he read what she had so faultlessly typed. 'You were speaking the truth,' he observed admiringly, taking his eyes from the paper in his hands.

Strangely, she wanted to laugh. 'I never lie on a Friday,' she commented—and made hastily for the door.

She went to the kitchen wondering what on earth was the matter with her? She knew for a fact that some of the executives at Masters asked especially that she should do their work. Her pride and accuracy in her work was appreciated. Indeed, her employers said as much. But never, when receiving compliments from one of them, had she ever felt so flustered as just now, when Lukas Tavinor had intimated she had been speaking only the truth when she'd said she was brilliant at typing reports.

'Anything I can help you with?' she asked Mrs Dobson on going into the kitchen.

'That's most kind of you, but no,' the housekeeper declined. 'You were such a big help this morning, preparing the salad for lunch and doing the vegetables for tonight. Ash has taken your sister's tray up, so I can put my feet up for an hour or so. I've laid for lunch in the dining room.'

From preference Jermaine would have chosen to eat with the housekeeper. By the sound of it Edwina had no intention of leaving her room until this evening, which meant she would have to eat her lunch with Lukas and Ash—and she had nothing very much she wanted to say to either of them.

As it happened Jermaine wasn't called upon to say very much at all. Ash was solicitous and, while seeing to it that she had all to eat that she required, seemed to put himself out to entertain her. Jermaine wondered, had she not discovered he had 'feet of clay', if she would have been flattered by his attentions. Involuntarily she glanced at Lukas—and thought not. Somehow Lukas, who was saying very little but, she didn't doubt, missed nothing, seemed more of a man of the two—Ash, by comparison, seemed quite shallow.

Jermaine blinked and wondered at the way her thoughts were going. She'd never used to think of Ash as shallow. She had in fact been quite taken with him! But, now, she all at once felt quite grateful that Ash had defected. It endorsed for her the fact that they had been going nowhere and that their non-relationship would have eventually, sooner rather than later, petered out.

She looked at Lukas and found his eyes on her. She flicked her glance away as the craziest notion struck that, beside Lukas, any man would appear shallow. *Good grief!* Get your head together girl, do!

'More fruit?' Ash enquired.

Jermaine shook her head and, with a quick look at their empty plates, said, 'If you've both finished?' she took charge bossily, 'I'll clear this table and you...'

'I'll help,' Ash volunteered—Jermaine noticed 'Big Brother' stayed silent.

Lukas had gone by the time she returned from the kitchen with a tray. She was glad he had gone. She was feeling a touch unnerved and wasn't quite sure why. Though it was true she was hating this farcical situation she had been forced into.

She was busily stacking the tray with used dishes when, looking up, her glance lighted on Ash—she had never seen him looking so down.

'What's the matter, Ash?' she enquired quietly.

'Oh, sorry,' he apologised at once. 'I was trying not to let it show.'

'You're upset about something?'

He shook his head—but then, as if unable to keep it bottled up any longer, 'Edwina,' he said. 'I know she's in pain but—well, I arranged to have today off so I could be with her, so she wouldn't have to suffer alone, but she doesn't seem to want to know.'

Jermaine was at something of a loss to know what to say. She supposed she could have reminded him that with the roads being flooded he'd have had to take the day off anyway. But that wasn't the point. He was hurting and, knowing that Edwina was likely to ditch him any day now, Jermaine didn't see how she could give him false hope with regard to her sister.

'I'm—sorry,' was the best, the inadequate best, she could come up with, and she disliked it intensely that Edwina had put her in this position, where she couldn't give Ash the hope that everything would come out right for him.

'No, *I'm* sorry!' Ash exclaimed quickly. 'Whatever was

I thinking of, complaining to you after the shabby way I treated you?'

'Oh, Ash,' Jermaine said helplessly. But as he moved towards her, and she received the distinct impression that because he was so upset he was coming over to her for a hug of comfort, she quickly changed the subject. 'Come on,' she brightly donned her bossy hat again, 'Let's get these dishes back to the kitchen.'

Ash helped with a few chores in the kitchen—which was rare, she guessed, because Mrs Dobson seemed quite bemused by it happening. Not so Jermaine, for it became clear to her, when he asked her to go for a walk with him in the grounds of Highfield, that Ash was very much at a loose end.

'I've already been up to my ankles in your brother's grounds once today, thanks all the same,' she declined.

'I'm sure Mrs Dobson has a pair of wellingtons somewhere she can lend...'

'I'm mid-way through typing a report for Lukas,' Jermaine interrupted, and escaped from the kitchen, Ash already gone from her thoughts. How peculiar! For all Lukas's name had come out sounding quite natural, she had felt all kind of chaotic inside on speaking his name.

By the time she arrived at his study she was consigning any such nonsensical notion to the bin. Since she had started a precedent, she opened the door and went in without knocking.

Lukas Tavinor looked up as she entered. 'I'm back,' she said, unnecessarily, she knew, but she somehow felt the need to make some small comment—though why just seeing this man should make here feel all kind of out of step with herself, she was baffled to know.

She took her seat thinking he might have likewise made some pleasant reply. A 'So I see' wouldn't have hurt. But forget that, and forget pleasantry. He did have something to say, however, albeit more grated than said as he questioned toughly, 'What's with you and Ash?'

Taken slightly aback, Jermaine stared at Lukas wide-eyed. Talk about accusing! Where did he get off...? 'Nothing's with Ash and me!' she retorted hotly. 'Except in your imagination,' she added for good measure—and ignored him from then on, slamming into finishing the report, wishing she was the kind of person who could leave work only half done.

Pig! Watchful swine! Those keen grey eyes didn't miss much, did they? Not that there was anything very much to miss—except, she qualified, that perhaps she and Ash might seem to know each other that bit better than merely having been introduced once by Edwina. Trust eagle-eyed Lukas to notice. Though it wasn't so much what he said which she found so annoying as the way he said it. Arrogant devil!

An hour later and Jermaine found she had worked her anger with Lukas out of her system. A half-hour after that and, her respect for his work extremely high, she began printing off what she had that afternoon typed, and was once more on as much of an even keel as she was likely to be, given the circumstances.

The phone rang as she was collecting the papers together. She almost reached automatically for it. She checked, and left Lukas to answer it—only he didn't, and she realised he was too involved with what he was doing. Either that or he wasn't expecting a call and had left Ash or Mrs Dobson to take the call elsewhere in the house. But the ringing reminded her that she needed a telephone.

She inspected her work for mistakes, found none, but when she decided to leave her work by the computer for Lukas to pick up, a glance in his direction showed he had broken off from what he was doing and had his eyes on her.

'I think that's it,' she murmured calmly, taking her work over to him instead.

Lukas took the papers from her, scanned quickly through, and he too, by the sound of it, had recovered his temper, for it was pleasantly that he remarked, 'With people like you working for Masters, it's no wonder the firm's the success it is.'

Oh, my word—did he know how to turn on the charm when he felt like it! 'You don't have to go overboard—it was only a report,' she answered dryly, but needed a favour. 'Talking of telephones,' said she, quite well aware that they hadn't been, 'do you have one of the portable variety?'

He didn't bat an eyelid. 'You're thinking of taking a stroll down to the bench by the bridge and calling up a few friends?'

She almost smiled, but didn't. 'Edwina wants to ring our parents,' she replied, and made the mistake of looking into a pair of steady grey eyes which seemed to her to be clearly accusing, *I thought you didn't tell lies on a Friday.*

Lukas soon found her a phone and Jermaine took it upstairs, unable to again refrain from wondering—had he seen through Edwina? Oh, it would be just too shaming if he knew that there was nothing the matter with her—other than that she was after *him.* But what had that look in his eyes been all about when she'd asked about a phone? Did he know that Edwina had not the smallest intention of phoning her parents?

Jermaine went to her sister's room and found Edwina bathed and dressed and taking her ease on a sofa. She looked up from the magazine she was flicking through. 'Is Lukas still working?' Ash, Jermaine gathered, must have told Edwina that he was.

'He's still in his study,' Jermaine answered.

'How tiresome. I'm getting really fed up with this room.'

In Jermaine's view, it was a lovely room. 'There's nothing to stop your leaving it,' she reminded her.

'Not much! The minute I set foot downstairs Ash will be there, wanting to know what he's done wrong.'

'You've obviously started the "Don't ring me, I'll ring you" treatment, then,' Jermaine realised, and when Edwina didn't deign to answer Jermaine decided to do some ringing of her own. She dialled her parents' number.

'What are you doing?' Edwina screeched, plainly having a very good idea.

Jermaine ignored her, and, when her father at once answered the phone, said, 'Hello, Dad, it's Jermaine. Edwina's waiting to speak to you.'

'How is she?'

'She's fine.' And, walking over to the sofa, she continued, 'I'll put her on,' and held out the phone to her sister.

For a moment Edwina just sat there looking sulky and said not a word. But, when Jermaine was starting to think she might have to find some other way of getting her sister to speak to their father, Edwina snatched the phone from her with an angry, impatient movement. 'Hello, Daddy,' Edwina cooed, adopting her little-girl voice. 'Yes, I've been in very great pain...' Jermaine could have slapped her, worrying him like that. Though she felt marginally better when it seemed her father wanted to send a consultant to examine his elder daughter's back. 'What? A specialist? Here?' Edwina said, barely hiding her alarm. But, as quick as ever, she at once assured him, 'Oh, that won't be necessary. As Jermaine has said,' she went on, throwing her sister a venomous look, 'I'm fine now. Just a bit achy, that's...'

Jermaine didn't wait to hear any more. Edwina would hate her for about a week. That was the norm when, pushed beyond bearing, Jermaine sometimes retaliated. She went along to the room she had used last night. By the look of it, she was going to have to spend another night here.

She remade her bed, and, prior to going downstairs to collect her bag from the car, she popped into Edwina's room to collect the phone. Edwina wasn't speaking. Good. Jermaine didn't feel much like speaking to her either.

When she returned to her room she surveyed her scant wardrobe. Two shirts, the deep blue suit she had on, and some spare underwear. Edwina would have a whole wardrobe full of surplus clothes, but Jermaine wouldn't ask her. Instead she rinsed out yesterday's shirt and underwear, and knew she was going to have to settle for today's shirt to wear at dinner.

She took a shower and washed her hair, but was ready to go downstairs long before she heard sounds of Edwina being assisted down to the drawing room. It sickened Jermaine that Edwina could play-act in this way. Jermaine felt sick with herself too that, out of sisterly loyalty, she was having to go along with it.

When she was certain that the 'stretcher party' were safely downstairs and behind closed doors, she left her room and made for the kitchen to give what help she could.

Edwina was fit enough to come to the table for dinner, and had Jermaine, who knew her sister well, had any doubts about which Tavinor brother she was after, then those doubts disappeared into thin air as she watched her in action.

Here we go, Jermaine inwardly squirmed, wondering why neither Lukas nor Ash could see through Edwina's putting on the allure. But perhaps they could. Perhaps they were both too well mannered to notice it.

But, whether they had or whether they hadn't, Jermaine grew quieter and quieter with every breathless word Edwina spoke as, occasionally tossing a light remark to Ash—mustn't be entirely obvious, Jermaine observed—Edwina concentrated, in the main, solely on their host.

Their host, who was too sophisticated perhaps to give

her the put-down she deserved; too good-mannered, for the very reason that he was host, to tell her to go and bat her baby-blue eyes elsewhere. It could have been, of course, that he was answering all of Edwina's breathless questions with a certain degree of charm because he, like his brother before him, had fallen for her.

That thought gave Jermaine something of a jolt, and she darted a glance at him—to find he was looking her way. She averted her eyes. She didn't want to be here; she wanted to go back to her flat. She felt sick inside—and the only reason she could come up with to explain that was the notion that Lukas might be treating Ash in the same way that Edwina treated her; the notion that Lukas would have no regard for Ash if he felt like stealing Ash's girlfriend.

Yet she couldn't quite believe that of Lukas. She'd seen the way he and Ash were in each other's company. The greatest of friends. No, Lukas wouldn't... But, then again, what did she know? She was glad everybody had finished dessert. She wouldn't hang about for coffee. She'd go and see Mrs Dobson and then go straight to bed.

'I had a call from an estate agent this afternoon,' Ash announced generally, but Jermaine saw his eyes were on Edwina. 'He says he has the very property for me.' And, definitely addressing no one but Edwina, 'I'm going to view it tomorrow—do you think you'll be well enough to come with me?'

Jermaine willed her sister to say yes even while, if her assessment was correct, she knew full well that she wouldn't. 'Oh, Ash, I'm sorry,' Edwina answered, and managed to look it. 'I wouldn't be able to sit for that long.' To Jermaine's knowledge he hadn't said how long or how far away the property was! 'I know I'm sitting now,' Edwina added quickly, before anyone should remind her of that fact, 'but all that bumping along in a car... And in any case,' she went on, glancing down at the table, Ash no longer worthy of her 'special' look, apparently, '...according to what you were saying earlier today, the roads will be flooded for a few days yet, and we wouldn't be able to get out.'

In spite of the way Ash had behaved to her, Jermaine felt quite sorry for him. But as he went on to explain to Edwina, 'Lukas says I can borrow his Range Rover,' so Jermaine was too instantly furious to think of anyone but Lukas Tavinor. He had a Range Rover?

She stared at him, thunderstruck for the moment before her feeling of outrage peaked. 'You've got a Range Rover?' she exploded, flames of fury storming in her violet gaze. 'A *high off the ground* Range Rover? One that can go through floods?'

Lukas held her gaze, her fury not lost on him for all that his voice was mild as he calmly replied, 'It's advisable to have one in this area.' He smiled, the swine, he actually *smiled!* 'If we're not rained in, we're snowed in,' he explained pleasantly.

Jermaine drew breath, ready to go for his jugular—but Edwina, an angel by contrast, was batting her eyes at him and trilling, 'But a price so well worth paying to live in this most heavenly of heavenly places.'

Jermaine knew her control was thin. If she didn't leave the room right now she'd be throwing something at Lukas. She didn't bother saying goodnight—stuff manners—but jerked out of her chair and went quickly from the dining room. To think she had been stuck there all day when Tavinor could have given her a lift to the railway station! Instead of which she'd had to stay cooling her heels while the work on her desk piled up. And, to add insult to injury, instead of being at her job doing *her* work—she had been hard at it in his study, doing *his!*

Oh, it was intolerable! He had a Range Rover, parked, ready, waiting, doing nothing! She wouldn't mind betting he had never intended to go to his office but, even before the storms of Thursday, had planned to work from home today. Had he *wanted* to go to his office that day, the Range Rover would have got him there—anyone else, forget it!

CHAPTER FOUR

As soon as it was light enough to see out the next morning, Jermaine was at her window. She sighed—there was still too much water about for her to risk driving her car, indeed, it would be the height of folly to try to drive through the floodwater. She felt defeated even as she tried to tell herself that Saturday was not a work day and that there was no urgency for her to leave.

There was no urgency to leave to get back to her job, she amended, but there was an urgency to leave. While it was true she had been invited to Highfield, because of Edwina's play-acting Jermaine was very aware that she was there under false pretences.

But—that wasn't her fault, she rallied. She'd tried hard to avoid coming to Highfield. In fact she'd done her very best *not* to. But, no, his lordship wasn't having that, was he? Well, it was his fault, not hers, going to see her parents the way he had, she fumed.

He'd just jolly well have to put up with it! Let him deal with having his home invaded. Not that she'd even intended to stay one night, much less two. Jermaine stared helplessly out from the window. If this little lot didn't clear up today, she could be there a *third* night.

But *he* had a Range Rover! Jermaine played for a while with wonderful wild thoughts of taking a temporary loan of the vehicle—in the circumstances she didn't care to term it stealing. Two things were against that, however. For one thing she had no idea in which of the probably locked out-buildings the four-wheel drive was garaged, and for another she just hadn't a clue how one started such a vehicle without a key.

She admitted she was not feeling at her most cheerful as she headed down the stairs. But, since the housekeeper was the only one Jermaine considered blameless in all of this, she pinned a smile on her face when she went into the kitchen. 'Good morning, Mrs Dobson,' she greeted her brightly. Though she was very tempted to let Edwina go without breakfast, she set about making her some.

Jermaine returned to the kitchen after she had delivered the breakfast tray, and spent the next twenty minutes assisting where she could, before the housekeeper assured her she could cope very well now.

Jermaine would have been happy to have had her breakfast in the kitchen, only just then Ash came looking for her. 'Now, why did I think you'd be here?' He smiled. 'Come and join me for breakfast,' he insisted.

By the sound of it Lukas wasn't at breakfast. Good. Jermaine left the kitchen with Ash, but when she preceded him into the breakfast room she saw that three places had been laid at the table—one of them already occupied.

Lukas Tavinor wasn't her favourite person just then. She would have ignored him, though found it difficult when, his grey eyes steady on hers, he enquired pleasantly, 'Over your little tantrum?'.

Ooh, was he asking for a thump! She glared at him for his trouble, but otherwise ignored him anyway. Ash, who seemed to be in a world of his own all of a sudden, pulled out a chair at the table for her. Too late now to wish she had stayed in the kitchen.

Quite inexplicably, Jermaine found she suddenly felt tongue-tied. Her? It was almost as if she was shy. Shy? Oh, for heaven's sake! Shy of what? The elder Tavinor, who was sitting there, totally unconcerned, eating his breakfast?

Ash, who was quiet all at once—as if he had a lot on his mind?

Jermaine helped herself to some toast from the toast rack, but looked up when Ash called her name. 'Jermaine,' he said again, his look somehow pensive. 'You wouldn't care to come and have a look at this house I'm going to see this morning—would you?'

Jermaine didn't think she *would* care to. On the other hand, what else was on offer but to stay at Highfield, kicking her heels while she waited for the road conditions to improve? She was still undecided, however, when for no reason she glanced at Lukas. Oh, my word! Grey eyes, highly disapproving, bored into hers. She remembered Lukas yesterday, his grated 'What's with you and Ash?', and a defiant light entered her eyes.

She turned from Lukas and smiled at Ash. 'I'd love to,' she answered. Perhaps he'd drop her off at some nearby railway station afterwards. 'What time are we going?' Lukas Tavinor, obviously having sufficiently breakfasted, left the breakfast room without saying another word. No doubt, Jermaine mused sourly, he thought her place was there, taking care of her sister. Tough!

Jermaine did look in on Edwina before she went, however, and found Edwina had roused herself to eat some of her breakfast. The room was a mess, so while her sister lounged in bed Jermaine set to tidying it and putting Edwina's discarded clothes away.

'I'm going with Ash at eleven to view the property the agent phoned about,' Jermaine informed her—and didn't miss the way Edwina's eyes lit up at the prospect of having Lukas to herself for a while.

'Don't hurry back,' Edwina instructed, and, having a lot to do if she was to be stunning by eleven, she got out of bed and headed to inspect her wardrobe. 'Come to think of it, don't come back at all,' she further instructed.

'I suppose it's not your fault that you're so unbearable!' Jermaine commented tartly.

'Dad should have taken his belt to me,' Edwina agreed, and because Jermaine loved her despite all she just had to laugh. 'Keep Ash out as long as you can, will you?' Edwina requested seriously.

Jermaine sobered. Poor Ash. 'You're impossible,' she told her sister candidly, and left Edwina to make herself ready for her five past eleven onslaught on the master of Highfield.

The house which Jermaine went with Ash to see was some twenty miles distant. At the start of their journey, there seemed to be water everywhere. But, for all it was a gloomy, overcast kind of day, the roads further on were dry as they left the flooded area behind.

Mr Fuller, the estate agent, was waiting for them when they arrived at the attractive four-bedroomed residence. After he had shown them from room to room he left them so they should look over the property on their own.

It was a very nice property, but in Jermaine's opinion it didn't have the charm of Highfield. There was, she reluctantly had to admit, something rather special about Highfield. Too good for its wretched owner, anyway. Now why did she have to think about *him?*

'What do you think?' she asked Ash quickly, for some reason not wanting to dwell on thoughts of Lukas Tavinor.

They were inspecting the upstairs rooms when she asked her question. But Ash stopped dead and turned, and Jermaine nearly cannoned into him. 'I think Mr Fuller thinks you and I are contemplating setting up home together,' Ash answered quietly. Taking a hold of her arms, he tried to draw her close. 'Oh, Jermaine,' he exclaimed miserably, 'how I wish he was right.'

Good heavens! Jermaine stared at Ash in amazement. 'Aren't you forgetting a little something?' she reminded him, resisting the pressure he was using to take her in his arms. 'A little something by the name of Edwina?'

'These last couple of days—ever since you arrived—I've started to see that Edwina isn't the one I want,' Ash stated. The old Ash was suddenly there as he smiled his old smile—and Jermaine was appalled. She'd used to love his little-boy smile. What had happened to her? Now, instead of smiling back, she felt only irritation with him.

His head started to come down. She moved her head out of range, and his kiss landed on her cheek. 'Don't you dare!' She pushed him impatiently away. Ash stared at her, his expression changed from smiling to astonished as she angrily fumed, 'What the dickens do you think I am?'

'I've offended you? Oh, Jermaine, forgive me, I never intended to do that. I never...'

'Give me the keys—I'll wait in the Range Rover!' she demanded shortly.

'Jermaine, I...' She held out her hand for the keys. But Ash had seen all he wanted to of the property, it seemed. 'I'll come with you,' he said.

They were silent on the way back, save for Ash once trying to explain that it had come to him last night that he had made one colossal mistake, and that he had allowed lust to rule his head. He also tried to explain that it was only when he'd seen Jermaine beside her sister that he'd...

'I am *not* interested,' Jermaine cut him off. 'And if you have any regard for me at all, you'll just shut up.'

After that, all was quiet on the return journey to Highfield. Jermaine owned she was not over her annoyance with Ash—and it had nothing to do with his defection but everything to do with the fact that any man should believe he could pick her up, and drop her down, and then think she would be grateful when he tried to pick her up again. He had even attempted to kiss her!

The journey back didn't seem to take as long as the

outward journey, and they were at Highfield before Jermaine recalled she had been thinking of asking Ash to drop her off at the nearest railway station.

'Jermaine, I...' Ash began, turning to her as he halted the Range Rover at the top of the drive.

'Forget it, Ash,' she cut him off. She didn't think she was cross with him any longer—just plain weary of the whole messy business. With that, feeling down, she left Ash to garage the vehicle and walked over the drive and indoors.

What she didn't need in the mood she was in was to have Lukas Tavinor come out of his study just as she was passing the door. If he'd been watching for her from the windows, he couldn't have timed it better.

But one glance at his unfriendly expression was all Jermaine needed to know that their meeting was accidental—her sister's efforts in her absence didn't appear to have put him in the sunniest of moods, Jermaine observed. She began to feel more cheerful.

She had intended to walk by him without a word, but then discovered she had been wrong in her belief that, likewise, Tavinor had nothing he wanted to say to her either. Because, before she had taken more than two steps, his right hand suddenly snaked out and caught hold of her right arm—and the next she knew she found he had pulled her into his study and slammed the door shut.

Jermaine was gasping at how fast it had happened, but as he let go her arm it wasn't very long before she gained her second wind and was ready to pitch into him in no uncertain terms.

Before she could, though, *he* was going for *her* main artery. 'The reason you're here is for your sister's benefit, not my brother's!' he clipped aggressively.

Jermaine's jaw fell open from the shock of this onslaught. 'You obviously didn't care to play nursemaid in my absence!' she slammed straight back.

'Ash is your sister's boyfriend!' Lukas reminded her grimly.

So he'd noticed? 'She's welcome to him!' Jermaine retorted—what in blazes was all this about?

'You're not moving in with him?'

She stared at him thunderstruck. 'Because I've been to see a property with him?' she questioned, astounded.

'There's more going on with the two of you than that!' Lukas gritted aggressively. 'I saw the way he greeted you when you arrived. Yesterday he was all over you, and you haven't hurried back today, so don't tell me there's nothing between you...'

'Oh, for heaven's sake!' Jermaine exploded. 'What is it with this family?'

Lukas stared at her—and Jermaine knew she had said more than was wise. He was clever, was Lukas Tavinor—he'd work it out. 'You've had a spat with Ash?' he questioned, right on target.

'He—annoyed me,' she admitted.

'How?'

Jermaine glared at Lukas Tavinor. He cared not but waited, determined, it seemed, to have an answer. She went to sidestep him and open the door—he was there first.

'So, what's with you and Ash?' he demanded.

She sent him a seething look of dislike, but could tell he wasn't going to let up until she told him. 'If you *must* know,' she snapped, 'Ash was my boyfriend to start with.'

It was humiliating to have to confess that. But, when she had been expecting something sarcastic in the line of 'either you've got it or you haven't' in relation to Ash dumping her in favour of her sister, Lukas said nothing remotely like it, but rendering Jermaine very near speechless, his look

toughened, and it was harshly that he gritted, 'You're saying Ash had you between the sheets first?'

'I'm...' She was flabbergasted. 'Well, that *would* be the
way your mind works!'

'He didn't?'

'Look here...' she began angrily, feeling sorely like
bashing his head in. 'It...'

'How long were you and Ash going out?' he cut in,
staying with his theme to challenge.

'Three months!' she answered furiously—then, remembering the last two weeks of her and Ash, 'Maybe a little
less, but...'

'And in all that time you and he never...?' he began
sceptically. But Jermaine had had enough.

'Look here, you!' she flared, 'Not all women *do*.' That
made him raise his eyebrows.

'You—don't?' he questioned disbelievingly.

'I don't!' she flared. 'Honestly!' she huffed. 'I don't
know why I'm still standing here having this conversation
with...'

'Well—I'll be... You—haven't—ever?' he double-
checked.

'I didn't know it was compulsory!' she answered furiously.

He continued to stare at her for a few seconds. And then,
unbelievably, she saw his expression soften. 'You're
scared?' he probed gently.

She didn't want him gentle—it undermined her anger. 'I
haven't met the right man yet!' she tossed at Lukas airily—
and saw him smile.

'Oh, get thee behind me, Satan,' he said softly, his mean-
ing obvious—he saw her answer as a challenge!

'Fat chance!' Jermaine scorned, and, giving him a dis-
gusted look, went to push him out of the way of the door.
But only to find, when he caught a hold of her and her

heart started to beat erratically, that he wasn't ready to let her go yet. But as she looked into his eyes, her heart started thundering. There was mischief there, and teasing, and, staggeringly, his head was coming closer. She panicked.

'You're as bad as your brother!' she railed—that sent the teasing look on its way.

'Did Ash kiss you while you were out?' Lukas demanded stonily.

'Tried!' Jermaine snapped. '"Tried" being the operative word—it landed on my cheek.'

For no reason she could think of, his good humour appeared to be restored. 'Oh, naughty Jermaine,' he teased. 'Did you give him a set-down.'

Her lips twitched at the old-fashioned expression. She didn't want to laugh. No way did she want to laugh. But there was just something about this wretched man that had her doing things she didn't want to.

His glance went to her mouth. 'You're lovely,' he said. 'And even lovelier when you laugh,' he added, and, leaning down, he gently kissed her.

Something was trying to tell her that she shouldn't be standing there allowing him to kiss her. But as his lips touched hers and a tingling kind of sensation washed through her, right down to her toes, so her senses seemed to go absolutely haywire. She was still standing there when Lukas pulled back and looked into her eyes. She looked back, feeling mesmerised—what a wonderful, tender, absolutely sensational mouth he had.

How long she would have stayed there, just standing there staring at him, had he not been the first to move and break the spell she was under, Jermaine had no idea. But he did move, to kiss her again, and, even while a pounding started in her ears, Jermaine somehow managed to get herself more of one piece.

'I—er...' she mumbled, drawing back out of reach and

voicing the first excuse she could think of—though why she should need an excuse she had no idea. 'I'm—er—going for a shower,' she mumbled.

His hand went down to the door handle, but she didn't miss the sudden wicked light in his eyes when, just before he opened the door he enquired nicely, 'Want company?'

'Our requirements are different,' she answered as coolly as she could. 'I'm for a hot shower—I suggest you take a cold one!' His laugh followed her from the room.

Her lips twitched too, so she was glad she had her back to him as she crossed the hall and sailed up the stairs—but she was still staggered. What was it about the man? He seemed to be doing most peculiar things to her.

Up in her room she convinced herself that she didn't find him in the least bit funny. She was not amused. What she was, was stuck here—stranded—and he had a vehicle that would get her out. Against that, of course, there was pride. She wouldn't ask him, she'd be hanged if she would. And, anyway, why was she getting so stewed up? She would need her own vehicle to get her to work on Monday. Just supposing she did leave here in the four-wheel drive, she would only have to make a special trip back to collect her car.

Chafing against force of circumstance, Jermaine joined Edwina and the Tavinor brothers for lunch—and grew more and more embarrassed at Edwina's less than subtle attempts to ensnare Lukas. True, both he and Ash were polite to Edwina as she twittered breathlessly away. But, from Jermaine's point of view, if it was a fact that Ash had switched his allegiance back to her, then he most probably no longer wanted Edwina in his brother's home.

Which made it all rather splendid, didn't it? Lukas wanted neither of them here at Highfield, and the same went for Ash. Intolerable? It was beyond that. With her pride battered, Jermaine glanced at Lukas, her gaze falling on his splendid mouth. So, okay, he hadn't made a meal of it, but he had kissed her and... Her heart missed a crazy beat at the memory of his tender, gentle kiss.

She flicked her glance upwards—and to her consternation saw that Lukas was watching her. She went scarlet when, every bit as if he could read her mind and knew her every thought, Lukas Tavinor smiled.

Jermaine was back to hating him again and was silently calling him a swine. She was glad that he wasn't at dinner that night, and had fresh reason to hate him that he—he with his transport—could go out, leave the house whenever he chose. No doubt he was out somewhere, wining and dining with *Beverley!*

Jermaine did not sleep well that night and was showered and dressed early. As soon as it was light enough to see outside she was off down the stairs. As soon as she was able, she was leaving.

Her first port of call, however, was the kitchen, where she found the housekeeper having her first cup of tea of the day. 'Will you join me?' Mrs Dobson invited, heading for the teapot.

'Not just now, Mrs Dobson.' Jermaine smiled. 'But if you've a pair of wellingtons I may borrow to take a look around?'

Ten minutes later, dressed in a pair of wellingtons and an over-large, heavy topcoat, which the housekeeper was certain Jermaine would 'catch her death' without, Jermaine was going quickly down the drive to take a look at the road beyond.

There was still plenty of water about, she observed, but not so much. Good—she was going to risk it. Strangely, Jermaine felt a most decided pang at the thought of leaving Highfield. Then wondered, why shouldn't she? It was a lovely house, not to say a beautiful house, and since it was most unlikely she would ever set foot here again, to feel that little twinge of regret was only natural, surely?

She wouldn't feel the slightest pang at saying goodbye to its owner, though. Nor would she feel any anguish at the thought of never seeing him again. But, manners being manners, she would thank him for his hospitality—and get out of there.

Though first... Somehow Jermaine felt pulled to go and look again at that idyllic spot by the little footbridge. Unable to deny that pull, she made her way to the rear of the house and then to the small wooden bridge, where the waters beneath were much less of a tiny torrent now than they had been.

Because she couldn't resist it, Jermaine went over to the bench and sat down, and for some moments enjoyed the peace, tranquillity—quiet solitude.

She was, however, just feeling grateful that Mrs Dobson had insisted she borrow her topcoat, when her quiet solitude was broken by the sound of someone approaching.

'I thought it was you—even if I did recognise the coat,' Lukas Tavinor commented as she turned.

'Mrs Dobson loaned it to me—and the wellingtons,' Jermaine answered.

'Why wouldn't she?' Lukas smiled. 'You're her favourite.'

Favourite! Jermaine stared at him. 'Me? Why?'

'According to Mrs D, you've been more than pulling your weight. You've seen to it that your sister has breakfast in bed.' Guiltily Jermaine remembered how yesterday she had been in two minds about letting Edwina 'starve.' 'She says you've also made sure that neither of you need trouble her. You're always cheerful and friendly, and eager to do any small task, no matter how menial. You're...'

'Stop! I can't live up to this,' Jermaine cut in, and, wanting to change the subject, she honestly told him, 'I could quite miss this wonderful spot.'

She wasn't sure what she expected him to say, but it certainly wasn't his sharp, 'You're thinking of going somewhere?'

His tone annoyed her. It had no place in this enchanting spot. 'In half an hour!' she answered bluntly.

'You can't!' he rapped.

'Watch me!' she tossed back. 'And thank you for your hospitality.'

He threw her a murderous look, clearly not wanting her thanks, and her pleasant mood evaporated. He had spoiled everything. Without another word, Jermaine got up and left him.

Lukas Tavinor was nowhere around when, a little over half an hour later, Jermaine put her overnight bag in the back of her car. Ash was, and came out to her car with her.

'You'll drive carefully, Jermaine,' he instructed.

'Don't I always?'

'There'll probably be a lot of debris around after the flooding.'

'I know. I'll be careful.'

'Jermaine.' She looked at him. 'May I kiss you goodbye?' Ash asked.

She suddenly felt sorry for him. And yet, oddly, when they had kissed in the past and she had quite enjoyed his kisses, she didn't want his mouth against her own now. She was sure it had nothing to do with the fact that his brother had yesterday kissed her—and she had tingled all over. Good grief! This enforced incarceration at Highfield must have turned her brain. But, in any event, she offered her cheek to Ash.

'Goodbye, darling. Take care,' he said, and saluted the cheek she offered.

As soon as she arrived at her flat she telephoned her

parents. She did her best to assure them that there was little the matter with Edwina—naturally her father thought Jermaine was being very hard-hearted. Her mother, however, was for once slightly ascerbic, remarking, 'Edwina always did have the flu longer and much worse than anyone else in the area,' causing Jermaine to realise that their mother saw more than she'd been aware. How much longer Edwina was going to continue playing the martyr down at Highfield was anybody's guess. Highfield…

Jermaine was glad to be extra-busy the next day. The hours she had spent at Highfield seemed to have disturbed her more than she'd appreciated. At any unsuspected moment she would find herself thinking about more or less everything that had taken place since giving in to coercion last Thursday and driving down to Lukas's home. She thought about Edwina, who didn't want Ash. And about Ash, who apparently no longer wanted Edwina. Though, mysteriously, Jermaine found she was thinking more about Lukas than any of them. Lukas, who was a law unto himself and, by the look of it, didn't want anybody.

Two days later, Jermaine was so busy at her office she didn't have time for lunch. But, having at last caught up, she left work on time and reached her flat to hear her phone ringing. Lu… Abruptly she strangled the thought before it could go further. Just because Lukas Tavinor knew her phone number—just because he was in her head a lot just lately—it didn't mean he was going to call her.

Heavens above—as if she wanted him to! She picked up the receiver. 'Hello,' she said, and heard Stuart Evans, her friend and work colleague, asking her how she felt about keeping him company at the nearby Chinese restaurant.

'We needn't stay late,' he added.

'Which means that there's football on one of the TV channels at nine o'clock,' she interpreted, and owned she didn't feel much like cooking a meal for herself. 'I'll meet you there in half an hour?' Stuart lived a few streets away in an apartment the company had likewise found for him.

'I'm passing your door—I'll pick you up in ten.'

He was obviously starving. Jermaine freshened up a little and ran a comb through her shoulder-length platinum-blonde hair. She was ready when Stuart drew up outside.

He was uncomplicated and easy to get along with, was Stuart. She had dated him a couple of times, but when she'd told him plainly that she wasn't interested in anything but friendship, he, unlike one or two others she had said the same thing to, had accepted it. That was when they had become friends.

'I asked you—my treat,' he said when she drew her purse from her bag. 'You can pay next time.'

Since she knew that she might well call him next week and invite him to keep her company at the local Indian restaurant, she put her purse away and Stuart drove her home. Equality of the sexes aside, Stuart got out of his car at her flat and saw her to her door, as he always did.

He watched while she opened the door, then gave her cheek a friendly kiss. ''Night, Jermaine,' he bade her.

'Enjoy your football,' she bade him, and they both laughed.

Jermaine watched in the light of the streetlamp as he pulled away, and had turned back to her door when, making her very nearly jump out of her skin, a curt voice demanded, rather than asked, 'Who was that?'

She spun about. Lukas Tavinor! Where the...? What...? She got herself together, the question of where he had sprung from fading as, regaining her composure, she offered sarcastically, 'You should have come out of the woodwork sooner—I'd have introduced you.'

Her sarcasm was wasted. 'Is he the reason you didn't want Ash to kiss you?' Lukas questioned toughly.

She'd had enough of him—and they were on *her* territory. 'If you've got a report you want typing—forget it!' she bristled.

He smiled and she could feel herself weakening. 'I could do with a cup of coffee,' he hinted.

And there was such charming persuasiveness in his voice that Jermaine found she had answered, 'So could I,' and had invited him to, 'Come up,' before she'd had time to think about it.

How long had he been there? she wondered as he followed her inside the building. And why, when she had climbed these stairs hundreds of times, was her heart pounding so? She had *run* up them sometimes, if she'd felt like it, and had never experienced such inner commotion.

'Come in,' she called over her shoulder as she opened the door of her small flat, suddenly realising that her meal must have restored her flagging energy. After a hectic day, she had been feeling a degree or two weary, but now, all at once, she felt brimful of vim and vigour. She put her bag down and went into the tiny kitchen. There was barely room for two and he was tall and broad-shouldered. 'I'll bring the coffee through,' she commented pointedly, when he followed her.

'I make you nervous?'

She gave him her best cool look. 'Not remotely,' she replied, and remembered to smile pleasantly as she added, 'This place isn't big enough for both of us.'

Jermaine was glad when he strolled to her sitting room; she realized, as she reached for a couple of cups and saucers, that her hands were shaking. Oh, get yourself together, do, she instructed herself impatiently. Why, she didn't even like the man half the time! In fact she quite hated him sometimes, so why on earth was she getting into this state?

Had he just finished work? Had he eaten? She popped her head round the sitting room door. Lukas was standing casually eyeing a rather expensive piece of porcelain she had always loved and which her mother had insisted she brought to the flat with her. 'Er—do you need a sandwich?' Jermaine enquired jerkily. For goodness' sake—if he were hungry he'd go and eat!

For a moment he looked at her speculatively. Then he smiled. 'I grabbed something earlier,' he replied, but added, 'You're rather a nice person, aren't you?'

Jermaine dived back into her kitchen. Nice! *Nice!* Who wanted to be *nice?* Nice, safe, predictable. She poured two cups of coffee, heartily wishing she had never issued an invitation for him to 'come up'.

Lukas relieved her of the tray when she carried the coffee in. Perhaps he liked to drink it scalding hot and wouldn't be but a few minutes, she hoped. 'Your friend obviously has an early start tomorrow,' he remarked, to confuse her totally.

'Sorry?'

'Your escort just now.'

'Stuart…' Light dawned—though she had no intention of explaining Stuart. 'You're working late?' she enquired. Or was he killing time before going on to meet someone? 'Why are you here?' she asked bluntly on that thought, belatedly wondering why the dickens she hadn't asked that question before. It was his fault; she blamed him, he confused her.

He smiled congenially, and she didn't like the feeling that he knew every thought that went through her head. 'In answer to your first question, I've stayed at my desk clearing any loose ends prior to flying to Sweden early tomorrow morning.' Jermaine refused to smile back and he took a drink of his coffee, and then went on, 'In answer to your second question, and since I won't be back until Friday afternoon, I thought I'd stop by on my way home to see how you felt about coming with me to an art exhibition on Friday evening.'

Jermaine was little short of amazed. He had called, in person, to ask her for a date? 'I wouldn't dream of coming with you,' she replied coolly.

'Don't prevaricate—tell me straight,' Lukas tormented.

She had been determined not to smile. Her lips twitched. He was impossible. 'I thought you were taking Beverley?' Jermaine reminded him sharply.

He looked amused. 'Did you?' he answered, which was no answer at all other than it told her that he felt it was nothing to do with him if she had misinterpreted the arrangements she had heard him making over the telephone. Even though Jermaine was sure he had been arranging to take Beverley to some art gallery or other this Friday.

'Huh!' Jermaine puffed. 'I fully appreciate it's unheard of for anybody to turn you down, but in case you didn't fully comprehend my answer the first time, no thanks.'

Sarcasm hadn't dented him, and neither did her repeated refusal. 'Oh, come on, Jermaine, you know you love art.'

She stared at him. She barely knew him, yet he seemed to know so much about her. 'Who told you I do?' she asked, and he looked long into her violet eyes, and Jermaine owned—she was weakening.

'I have an instinct about these things. Say you'll come, and I'll go to Sweden a happy man.'

His look, his smile, his charm, were potent forces. But, even so, she was ready to refuse a third time. And, what was more, she knew he was expecting her to. Then, oddly, at that precise moment, she thought of 'nice, safe, predictable', and something came over her. When she knew that Lukas was fully expecting her to again refuse, some inner rebel against 'nice, safe, predictable' rose up and refused to be pushed down. 'Well...' she began. 'Well, I suppose I can't really let you go to Sweden an unhappy man.'

Lukas was on his feet—if he was surprised, hiding it well. 'That was a definite "yes," if ever I heard one,' he stated, adding swiftly, 'I'm going before you change your mind.' Jermaine went with him to the door and, as if he couldn't resist, he gazed into her violet eyes for a moment and then dropped the lightest of butterfly kisses on her mouth.

He had gone before she could protest. But whether she would have done so or not Jermaine was hard put to it to tell. She seemed to be breaking all her own rules since knowing him.

She, who had a most decided aversion to being treated as second best, had—when clearly Beverley, the *numero uno,* must have broken a leg or something, and couldn't see Lukas on Friday—had accepted to be just that. She had accepted to go in her place.

She had made a date with him—and Edwina would hate her because of it.

She, Jermaine all at once realised, had—to crown it all—made a date with a man who, when she had as good as told him that she was a virgin, had as good as told *her* that he saw her as a challenge!

She should be wary of him; she knew she should. And yet all she felt was tremendously excited at the thought of seeing him again in two days' time. Oh, what on earth was happening to her?

CHAPTER FIVE

EVEN though she was extremely busy the next day, Jermaine found that thoughts of Lukas Tavinor still kept coming into her head. As common sense reasserted itself she knew she should never have accepted his invitation for tomorrow evening. What on earth had she been thinking of? So okay, she'd objected to being thought nice, safe and predictable, but where in blazes had her brain been?

And yet, five minutes later, she was wondering why in creation shouldn't she go to an art gallery with him? As he'd surmised, she did like art—well, most of it anyway.

Against that, though, she, who was never, ever going to be second best, had been Tavinor's second choice. Had to be. Beverley was his first choice—and must be severely incapacitated, since Jermaine was sure the gods decreed nothing less would prevent Tavinor going out with the first woman of his choice.

The phone on her desk rang. She answered it, discovered it was one of the newer executives, Nick Norris, phoning through about business. But, business done, he stayed on the line to ask her out the following evening.

'I'm—I've got something arranged for tomorrow,' she answered, and was aware—even if she could have got a message through to Lukas to cancel—that she was committed to going to the art gallery with him.

'Of course you have!' Nick accepted. 'It was a long shot, anyhow. But you're not engaged or anything like that, are you?'

Oh, crumbs. She liked Nick; his work was good and she seldom had problems with it. But she didn't know that she wanted to see him outside of a work environment. 'No, nothing like that,' she agreed slowly.

'You're going to tell me you're fully booked all next week?'

There had been a smile in his voice, and Jermaine wished she knew what the matter was with her, but she just didn't feel she wanted to go out with anyone just then. And it had nothing to do with the way Ash had behaved—two-timing her with her sister. But... Suddenly visions of his brother Lukas were in her head.

Heavens above, surely Lukas Tavinor wasn't the reason she didn't feel like dating anyone else! Oh, for goodness' sake, pull yourself together, do. 'Actually, Nick, with Christmas so close, I'm a bit pushed to find any spare time just now.'

'You must have the same large family I have,' he accepted. 'When there's only two weekends to go before Christmas, I've got three sisters all determined I should spend a weekend with them and their families when I deliver their Christmas presents. I don't suppose you'd care to...? No, I'm sure you wouldn't. I'll see you at the firm's Christmas dinner,' he promised. 'Are you bringing anybody, or...?'

'I'm going with Stuart,' she invented on the spot—and as soon as she'd said goodbye to Nick saw that Stuart had looked up from his desk.

'Where are we going?' he asked, having caught some of her conversation. 'And am I being used as an excuse?'

'Are you taking anyone to the staff dinner next Wednesday?' Jermaine asked.

'You, if you promise not to drink so I can?'

'You're on.' She laughed; she had been going to drive herself anyway. It would be no hardship to pick Stuart up and be his chauffeur for the evening.

Stuart went out of her head and she found she was wondering what Lukas Tavinor was doing next Wednesday. Which, to her way of thinking, was just *too* much. Anybody would think she wanted to ask *him* to partner her! Jermaine gave herself a severe talking-to.

Although, by Friday evening, she could not deny that she was feeling a little excited at the thought that at any moment now Lukas would call. She had been unsure what to wear, but in the end had opted for a deeply blue suit that enhanced the colour of her violet eyes.

For no reason, she felt dithery inside—and owned it was ridiculous. As it was ridiculous, she admitted—not for the first time in the see-saw of her thoughts—that she had accepted Tavinor's invitation in the first place. Again she gave herself a talking-to, and in the end decided that, provided she wasn't called upon to tell lies about her 'invalid' sister, she was going to enjoy the art gallery affair. In any event, it wasn't going to last more than an hour, was it? Just how long did it take to look at a few pictures?

Her apartment bell sounded. She swallowed, and was cross with herself that she did so. Picking up her dainty bag, she left her flat and went down the stairs. No point in inviting Tavinor up.

Ridiculously, she had to swallow again before she opened the door. She pinned a pleasant look on her face and felt her heartbeat quicken as she pulled back the door. 'Hello,' some actress addressed the tall, broad shouldered man standing casually there.

'Not a girl to keep a man waiting, I see,' Lukas remarked pleasantly, his grey eyes warm as he looked back at her.

'I thought it was raining,' she lied—as though she'd hurried to the door in case he might be getting soaked. 'How was Sweden?'

'Fine,' he answered as he escorted her to his car. 'Been busy?'

'Enjoyably so,' she replied, and sank down on to the

leather upholstery of his smart car. While Lukas went round to the driver's side, she felt the need to take a few deep and steadying breaths.

After her initial nervousness, however—and she could never remember being so uptight on a first date before; first and last she made a mental note—with Lukas keeping up a light conversation as they drove along, Jermaine began to relax. So much so that by the time they reached the art gallery, which was more or less one huge ground-floor room with a selection of movable partitions here and there, she was, as she had previously decided, all ready to enjoy the viewing.

'Lukas!' A short, slim, slightly intense-looking man broke away from the group he was with and came hurrying over as soon as he spotted them.

'How's it going?' Lukas asked, shaking hands with him.

'Fingers crossed—I've been in such a state!' the man confessed.

Lukas grinned, which Jermaine didn't think was very sympathetic of him. 'This is the man whose work you've come to admire,' Lukas said, turning to her.

'You're the artist?' she smiled, before Lukas could complete the introductions.

'Beverley Marshall,' he answered, and Jermaine's smile became a grin too—though she wouldn't look at Lukas. He knew darn well she had thought Beverley was a female, while of course Beverley could be a man's name too.

'Jermaine Hargreaves,' she supplied, and shook hands with him.

A hired waiter hovered near and Beverley called him over. Jermaine opted for a Buck's fizz and nursed her drink as the three of them fell into conversation.

It was not long, however, before people who appeared to know Lukas came up to them, and, the art exhibition a side issue, by the look of it, they seemed prepared to chat in a group all evening.

'You'll excuse us,' Lukas murmured suavely after a few minutes. 'There's one picture in particular I'm interested to see.'

Jermaine never discovered which picture that was. What she did discover was that there was one picture in particular that caught *her* eye. She was moving around the room with Lukas, stopping before each picture, sometimes making a comment, sometimes not, when they came to a pastel abstract entitled *Boy With A Barrow*. She could detect neither the boy nor the barrow at first, yet something about the picture appealed to her.

Lukas went to move on. 'You're impressed?' he enquired when she didn't move.

She stared at the painting. 'I can see a wheel,' she told 'nim eagerly as she spotted it.

'Where?'

'You don't believe me?'

'Sure I do. I just need to have your in-depth vision,' he explained.

'There.' Jermaine pointed to a fine swirl of red on the otherwise pale blue and pink canvas.

Lukas's eyes followed her finger. 'Didn't I say you had an artist's eye?' he smiled.

Jermaine laughed at his light humour and moved with him on to the next picture. Several people came over to them once they had been round the room. But when the conversation appeared to be more about business than anything else, and one of the wives took a couple of paces away from the group to study a nearby picture, it seemed a good idea to Jermaine that she should do the same.

Lukas was involved answering a point about which some man named Akerman had asked him when, believing she'd be back without Lukas ever having missed her, Jermaine casually meandered away. The picture she went to have a second look at, however, was not nearby.

Yes, that was most definitely a wheel, she decided, and stared fascinated at the blue and pink and the merging of a swirling wisp of red. She was sure the barrow was just coming into focus when she was suddenly aware that she was not looking at *Boy With A Barrow* alone.

'Something tells me you like this one more than any of the others,' Lukas observed.

'Give me long enough and I'll find the barrow and the boy,' she smiled. But, not wishing Lukas to think her rude, 'I didn't think I'd be missed for a few minutes.'

'You were away ten,' he informed her.

'You noticed me slipping away?' she asked, astonished, having thought him deeply involved in a business discussion.

'I may not have your eye for unscrambling abstract art, but I knew at once when the most beautiful woman in the room left my side,' he answered—and her heart crazily seemed to miss a beat.

She opened her mouth, sorely needing some witty retort, but found she was too stunned. 'There's no answer to that,' was the poor best she could come up with.

Shortly afterwards they were in conversation with Beverley Marshall again, and, having complimented him on his exhibition, Lukas said they were leaving. Whereupon, once she was seated in the car next to him, Jermaine discovered that her idea that she would spend about an hour with him and that once they'd left the art gallery that would be it was erroneous.

'I thought we'd eat at my club,' Lukas announced as he swung the car out into the traffic.

'I didn't know you were feeding me as well!' she exclaimed.

'You're suggesting I don't know how to treat a lady?' he teased.

Jermaine, having formed the very opposite view—that Lukas Tavinor knew all there was to know about women, and how to treat them—said nothing. She had to own that she had no objection to having dinner with him—she had been planning to have something on toast later anyhow.

His club—what she saw of it, apart from the dining room—was all leather furniture and antiques. 'What time did you arrive back from Sweden?' she enquired once they were seated, an innocent enough question, since she couldn't sit there all through dinner and say not a word.

'Late this afternoon,' Lukas answered as the waiter brought their first course; they were both starting with fish.

'You must have called for me straight from your office,' Jermaine realised—he must have gone from his plane to put in time at his desk. 'Have you had chance to relax at all?' she wondered. She worked hard, but the pace of his life seemed to leave hers standing.

'I'm relaxing now,' Lukas replied, his grey eyes holding hers.

She felt nervous and excited at the same time suddenly, and again wanted to say something witty. But all she could come up with was a dull, 'Good.'

'You've had a busy but enjoyable day too, you said?'

She shrugged. She had no intention of boring him out of his skull by telling him about work, so confined her answer to, 'Today's just flown by.'

'Have you worked for Masters and Company very long?'

'I worked for them in Oxford when I left school—at sixteen', she inserted. 'I stayed there four years then transferred to their head office here two years ago.'

'That makes you twenty-two.'

'Your maths teacher would have been proud of you,' she laughed, and felt all sort of squiggly inside when she saw he seemed to like the sound of her laugh—there was an upward curve on his breathtaking mouth anyhow. Breathtaking? 'How old are you?' she asked abruptly.

'Thirty-six,' he answered without hesitation. 'You're younger than your sister?'

She didn't want to talk about Edwina. To do so might mean she would be called upon to varnish the truth a little—and Jermaine felt then that she didn't want to lie to Lukas. 'That's right,' she said brightly.

'Edwina doesn't have a job—when she's well?' he enquired.

'Edwina—we—that is...' Lukas silently waited, and Jermaine started to wish she had told him she wasn't hungry and that she didn't require feeding. But too late now to wish, as well, that she had told him to take her back to her flat. 'At—er—one time... That is, my father didn't want either Edwina or me to do anything—er—work-wise, in particular. Um, we used to be quite... Well, we had money and...' She broke off. This was ridiculous! 'No,' she said bluntly, 'Edwina doesn't have a job.' Oh, heck, that didn't sound very good for Edwina. 'She's looking for the right opportunity,' she added, and looked straight into a pair of steady grey eyes... And you're it, she almost told him.

And could have hit him when he contributed, 'And meanwhile she has time on her hand in which to snaffle your men-friends?'

'Snaffle?' Jermaine repeated indignantly, not thanking him for referring to something which stung more because of Edwina's utterly disloyal trait than the fact that Ash had defected.

'Ash was your boyfriend first,' Lukas documented, when Jermaine refused to answer his question. 'Which explains why you were, naturally, reluctant to go down to Highfield to look after your sister.'

For the pure joy of letting him know just how wrong he'd got it, Jermaine was very much tempted to tell him that the reason she hadn't wanted to go to Highfield was because she had known full well that Edwina didn't need 'looking after'. That in fact there was absolutely nothing wrong with Edwina—other than that she'd got the master of the house in her sights. But, while Edwina had no qualms about being disloyal, Jermaine knew that she couldn't be the same. So she said nothing, but just glared stubbornly at him.

That was until, quite quietly, but, oh, so seriously, Lukas asked, 'Are you in love with my brother?'

Jermaine stared at him, and was quite dumbstruck to find an answer to his most unexpected question. 'Is that what this evening is all about?' she questioned tautly when she had her breath back. 'You looking after your brother's interests?'

It was Lukas's turn to stare at her, but he wasn't giving up on his question, she found, when he replied, 'I think Ash is quite big enough to look after himself. Are you?'

'Big enough to look after myself?' She had no intention of playing the game his way.

Lukas kept his gaze steady on her. 'Are you in love with him?' he insisted.

'He's a very nice person,' she prevaricated.

'Which means you're not in love with him,' Lukas decided; in Jermaine's view he was much too clever with his summing up. Though he was way off course, she realised, when he further reckoned, 'I've been stupid. Ash didn't prefer your sister over you—you were the one to do the honours.'

Was Lukas upset that she might have thrown his loved brother over? Jermaine didn't see how he could be. Not since he must have realised it hadn't taken Ash any time at all to turn his affections elsewhere.

'Strange as it may seem,' Jermaine replied loftily, 'you got it right the first time.'

'Ash told you on your last date...?'

She'd had enough. 'I don't want to talk about it,' she butted in bluntly.

'You're hurt! I'm...'

Jermaine shaking her head caused him to break off. 'Edwina's welcome,' she said and, determined to end this conversation, she glanced at his newly arrived main course and remarked, 'Your Beef Wellington looks better than my fricassee of chicken,' and had the shock of her life when, without more ado, Lukas swopped plates with her.

She went to protest, but instead burst out laughing, and, to her surprise, the mood immediately lightened. Lukas laughed too. And—she fell in love with him.

'Bon appetit,' he grinned, and her heart thundered.

'Likewise,' she said, and concentrated fiercely on her Beef Wellington, that or go to pieces. She couldn't love him, she barely liked him sometimes, but—love him she knew that she did. 'When are you going away again?' she asked, after some seconds of desperately searching for a safe topic.

'I've only just got back!' he protested

'I know.' She risked glancing up, her heart raced again. 'But Ash said—' or she'd thought he'd said—her brain seemed to be having an off few minutes '—that you were always jetting off somewhere.'

Lukas smiled, his grey eyes did too, and her heart flipped. 'So—I fly off again on Monday,' he said, and asked, 'What will you be doing while I'm away?'

'Nothing very much, I don't suppose,' she answered, and glanced from him to realise how feeble that sounded. She injected a little stiffening into her enfeebled backbone. 'Though, of course that depends how long you'll be away?'

'The soonest I can possibly make it back is Christmas

Eve,' Lukas replied, and, because she wanted to hear regret in his voice, she actually thought she heard it when he said that he'd be out of the country all that while—with no earthly chance of getting back to take her to another art gallery.

Get real! 'Ooh, I'll be doing more than nothing very much in all that time,' she laughed.

'Such as?'

She looked at him again, looked into his interested eyes, and went momentarily brain-dead again for some seconds. Grief, it sounded pathetic, but the only outing she'd got planned was the firm's dinner.

'Well, among other things,' she who hadn't wanted to lie to him lied cheerfully, 'there's the company's Christmas dinner next Wednesday...'

'You're taking a partner?'

Thank you, Stuart, wonderful Stuart. 'You almost met him,' she replied prettily.

'Stuart?'

Good heavens, he'd remembered Stuart's name? Though, on thinking about it, it wasn't that difficult a name to remember, and she had a sort of idea that Lukas forgot very little of anything.

'The same,' she replied.

'Are you serious with him?' he wanted to know, and, when Jermaine just sat and looked at him, 'Of course you're not,' he decided.

'Oh?' she questioned, not sure she cared for his calculations, even if they were accurate.

'While I can see that you owe Ash no allegiance whatsoever, I just don't see you as someone who'd be serious with one man and be out dining with another.'

He was right there, but she didn't thank him for it. Or, rather, she said, 'Thanks!' But didn't mean it.

'Now what have I said?' he teased.

'Add your last comment to a previous one of "nice",
and it all adds up to "dull",' she answered sniffily—and,
even if she did love him, could have thumped him when
he laughed.

'You dull? Never!' he decreed. 'You're beautiful and
charming, and far too spirited to ever be anything so me-
diocre as dull.'

Her heart fluttered—beautiful and charming? Oh, my
word! 'What are you having for pudding?' she asked.

'I'm not swopping this time,' he threatened, and she
laughed. Her world righted itself and the next half an hour
just flew by as they talked and smiled, talked and laughed,
and generally struck companionable sparks off each other.

They lingered over coffee and, because of her newly discovered love for him and the need she had just to be with
him, Jermaine could have lingered the night away with him.
But because of that love, and a pride that said he should
never know about it—though the way she was laughing or
smiling at his smallest quip he might soon guess—she knew
she had to put a stop to the evening.

'I've had a splendid time tonight,' she hinted.

She didn't have to say more. All too soon Lukas was
guiding her from the building, starting up his car—and pulling up near her door.

She thanked him. 'The art gallery was super.'

'Especially the *Boy With A Barrow*,' Lukas ribbed her
as he escorted her to the outer door of where she lived.

'It was rather a special picture. Well, I thought so anyway,' she added defensively.

'And you're quite right,' he agreed, taking her keys from
her and inserting one in the door-lock.

She wanted to invite him up. She didn't want the evening
to end. Lord knew when, if ever, she would see him again.
Surely it wouldn't hurt to invite him up for coffee? Pride,
girl, pride. Do you really want him to see, as surely he will

if you don't get your act together, exactly how you feel about him?

'We've just had coffee, so you won't want another,' she said as she turned to face him.

He laughed. 'You're wonderful,' he said.

'Now what did I do?'

'At the risk of sounding immodest, most women can't wait to get me inside to give me a cup of coffee.'

Oh, she did love him. She laughed too. 'Have a safe trip,' she bade him.

He took a step back and gazed at her, then, to her astonishment and joy, he asked, 'I don't suppose you'd consider coming up to Highfield tomorrow?'

He wanted her to go down to his home? Her heart thundered. She could see him again tomorrow. 'Er…' She murmured only slightly, not wanting to miss this quite unexpected but fantastic opportunity.

'I wouldn't ask, but unfortunately Edwina isn't sufficiently well to make her own bed yet—a back injury can be the very devil—and with you there to help, it would give Mrs Dobson a bit of a break,' Lukas explained.

Jermaine's heartbeat evened out. Idiot, idiot! You thought he was inviting you, personally. Oh, Jermaine, you fool!

'What do you say?' he pressed.

'What *can* a girl say?' Jermaine returned lightly.

She saw him smile, and she forgot totally about Edwina when Lukas further invited, 'And you'll stay the weekend?'

'Oh, I don't know about that,' she hedged, even while everything inside her screamed to accept. But, having hedged, she felt honour-bound to follow through with, 'I need to be back here on Sunday evening.'

'So you'll stay until after lunch on Sunday? Good,' he said, before she could get the words out to confirm. 'And you'll drive down in the morning?'

I'll come with you right now, her wayward heart cried.
'I'll come as soon as I can,' she answered soberly, and,
grabbing at a moment of sanity, opened the door. 'Goodnight,' she smiled.

But as she went to move away so Lukas took a step
closer, and as her heart began to race, so he took her into
his arms. She was barely breathing when his head came
down, and while the racing of her heart picked up yet more
urgent speed Lukas gathered her closer, and gently, linger-
ingly, and without hurry, he kissed her.

'Goodnight, Jermaine,' he murmured softly, and let her
go.

Blindly she turned from him and floated on auto-pilot up
to her small apartment. She had been kissed before, and
with more passion. But never had she been kissed so wonderfully, so beautifully, so—oh, his sensational mouth—so
sensationally, and—by the man she loved.

CHAPTER SIX

JERMAINE lay awake for hours just thinking of Lukas. She supposed she must have slept at some stage, but she awoke early and he filled her head again, and she was once more enthralled as she remembered his magical kiss

She was no more certain this morning quite why Lukas had invited her to go with him to the art gallery in the first place—not forgetting he had taken her to dinner afterwards. Yet she smiled as she thought—it hadn't been because he had been let down by any female named Beverley. Her smile became a grin. Lukas had known jolly well that she'd thought Beverley had been a female of the species.

Jermaine fell to pondering again why Lukas had asked her out. It couldn't have been purely to persuade her to go up to Highfield today to give Mrs Dobson some help. He could have done that when he'd called on Wednesday.

So why had he asked her out? Could it be—her heart started to beat energetically—that for all they had got off to a 'spikey' start, Lukas had come to like her a little?

Oh, she did hope so. Liking wasn't love, of course, but... Suddenly her heartbeat slowed down to a dull pattern. Grief, woman, have you forgotten? Edwina is in his home! Why would any man waste time with you when Edwina's around?

Stop that, do, Jermaine ordered, only then realising more fully how much Ash's defection in favour of her sister's charms had shaken her confidence. Jermaine decided there and then that Lukas had asked her out for no other reason than he *did* like her. Must do. Edwina was in his *home*, for goodness' sake! He hadn't been rushing back to her, had

The Harlequin Reader Service® — Here's how it works:

Accepting your 2 free books and gift places you under no obligation to buy anything. You may keep the books and gift and return the shipping statement marked "cancel." If you do not cancel, about a month later we'll send you 6 additional novels and bill you just $3.15 each in the U.S., or $3.59 each in Canada, plus 25¢ shipping & handling per book and applicable taxes if any.* That's the complete price and — compared to cover prices of $3.99 each in the U.S. and $4.50 each in Canada — it's quite a bargain! You may cancel at any time, but if you choose to continue, every month we'll send you 6 more books, which you may either purchase at the discount price or return to us and cancel your subscription.

*Terms and prices subject to change without notice. Sales tax applicable in N.Y. Canadian residents will be charged applicable provincial taxes and GST.

If offer card is missing write to: Harlequin Reader Service, 3010 Walden Ave., P.O. Box 1867, Buffalo NY 14240-1867

NO POSTAGE
NECESSARY
IF MAILED
IN THE
UNITED STATES

BUSINESS REPLY MAIL

FIRST-CLASS MAIL   PERMIT NO. 717-003   BUFFALO, NY

POSTAGE WILL BE PAID BY ADDRESSEE

HARLEQUIN READER SERVICE
3010 WALDEN AVE
PO BOX 1867
BUFFALO NY 14240-9952

Play The Lucky Hearts Game

and get...
FREE BOOKS & a FREE GIFT... YOURS to KEEP!

Scratch Here!
then look below to see
what your cards get you...

Yes! I have scratched off the silver card. Please send me my **2 FREE BOOKS** and **FREE MYSTERY GIFT**. I understand that I am under no obligation to purchase any books as explained on the back of this card.

386 HDL DC5Q																186 HDL DC5G

NAME   (PLEASE PRINT CLEARLY)

ADDRESS

APT.#   CITY

STATE/PROV.   ZIP/POSTAL CODE

Twenty-one gets you
2 FREE BOOKS and a
FREE MYSTERY GIFT!

Twenty gets you
2 FREE BOOKS!

Nineteen gets you
1 FREE BOOK!

TRY AGAIN!

Visit us online at
www.eHarlequin.com

Offer limited to one per household and not valid to current Harlequin Romance® subscribers. All orders subject to approval.

he? And, don't forget, he hadn't made a dash to get home as soon as he could after his Swedish trip, had he?

For a moment or two Jermaine dwelt on the blissful pleasure of realising that, when Lukas had known Edwina before he had known her, it was the younger Hargreaves sister he had chosen to spend time with. Did that signify, or did it not, that Lukas preferred her to Edwina?

Jermaine's bliss was short-lived when she recalled that for all she knew Lukas might think that Ash was in love with Edwina. While it was said that all was fair in love and war, Jermaine could not help but know that Lukas looked out for his younger brother. That being so, wouldn't Lukas perhaps deny his own inclinations and deliberately keep away from Edwina's charms—even if he did desire a closer liaison with her?

With her thoughts in more of a tangle than ever, Jermaine got out of bed, musing that the only thing she knew for sure was that while she had been strong enough to deny Lukas a cup of coffee last night, she had not been strong enough to deny herself the chance of seeing him, of perhaps spending some time with him today.

It was a little after eleven o'clock when, endeavouring not to be too eager while at the same time telling herself that the sooner she got to Highfield the sooner she would be able to give Mrs Dobson some assistance, Jermaine drove her car through the gates of Highfield.

An emotional tide of warm colour rushed to her face when, obviously on his way out for a walk or something of that nature, she saw Lukas step out onto the drive. Memory of his wonderful kiss swamped her.

He glanced down the drive and saw her and paused, waiting for her to pull up next to him. Jermaine was outwardly under control by the time he was opening the driver's door.

'I'm glad you're here,' he greeted her, and ridiculously, because she was sure he didn't mean anything by it, her heart leapt. He retrieved her overnight bag from the rear of the car. 'You're in the same room as last time,' he informed her pleasantly, and walked with her back inside the house.

Jermaine found her voice. 'Don't let me stop you from what you were doing.'

'Come down as soon as you've dropped off your bag. I'll get some coffee sorted,' he answered.

Was he going to have a cup of coffee with her? She felt all fluttery again at just the thought: the two of them, Lukas and her. 'I'll make it,' she determined. 'I'm not here to be waited on, and Mrs Dobson has enough to...'

'Mrs Dobson has Tina here to help her this weekend,' Lukas interrupted, stopping her dead, mid-flow.

'Tina?'

'Sharon's sister,' Lukas explained.

'Sharon—who helps Mrs Dobson during the week?' Jermaine remembered.

'Apart from the other Friday when Sharon's little boy was unwell,' he agreed.

Jermaine went to go on, but as she quickly realised that Tina's help must have been arranged in his absence, so Jermaine also very quickly realised that if Tina was there to assist Mrs Dobson today and tomorrow there was no reason at all for her being there. She stopped stock-still at the bottom of the staircase.

'You should have phoned me,' she protested. Oh, no, she was going to have to go back to London—and she didn't want to part from him, not yet.

'While it's always a delight to hear your voice, Jermaine, why did you want me to phone?' Lukas enquired, and Jermaine stared at him wide eyed.

'Why, to tell me not to come. With Mrs Dobson having all the help she requires, there's no need for me to be here,' she replied, promptly adding, 'I'll go.'

Lukas looked astounded. 'No, you won't!' he stated categorically, no ifs or buts about it.

'I won't? Why won't I?' Embarrassment that she was here at all under the circumstances made her voice short.

'Because...' he began to answer just as shortly, but then paused. Paused, and smiled, and said winningly, 'Because you type reports so absolutely accurately.'

Jermaine blinked, but a moment later was inwardly smiling. 'You rogue,' she admonished him nicely. 'You've a meeting before you fly off on Monday and you want your report on your Swedish trip typed and ready before then.'

He looked steadily at her, and then, making her tingle all over, he stroked a sensitive finger down her cheek—every bit as if he couldn't resist touching her. 'Say you will,' he coaxed.

She was seduced by him, seduced by his charm—and that was without the added bonus of being able to spend some time alone with him in his study. What could she do? 'Well, if you put it like that,' she replied sedately, joy just to be with him bursting in her heart.

'I'll rustle up that coffee,' he said decisively, and Jermaine again floated up a staircase.

Fearing her mood of high euphoria might be dampened if she saw Edwina, Jermaine sailed straight by her sister's door at the top of the stairs and went straight on to the room she had used that last time she had been at Highfield. She would look in on Edwina later.

It took Jermaine but a few minutes to unpack her overnight bag. But she took another couple of minutes in which she checked her appearance. Normally she wouldn't have bothered, but if Lukas was going to join her for coffee, and she rather thought he was, she needed the confidence-boost of knowing that she looked all right.

The mirror confirmed that her pale complexion was flawless, that her platinum-blonde hair needed no attention—

she ran a comb through it just the same—and that the small amount of make-up she had used looked all right.

That was as long as she could bear to be away from Lukas. Wanting to see him again, she hurried from her room—but only to bump into Edwina, limping from hers. Jermaine's feeling of excitement plummeted.

'Where on earth did you spring from?' Edwina, the first to recover, demanded.

Jermaine never had been fooled by the limp. 'How much longer are you going to keep this up?' she counter-demanded.

'Lukas is proving a tougher nut to crack than I'd antic-ipated,' Edwina answered, gladdening Jermaine's heart. But only to make her spirits dive when she added, 'But I see signs that he's cracking...' She broke off, and then, a cal-culating smile touching her mouth, she added 'I don't know why you're here, but since you are you can make yourself useful and take Ash off my hands—and leave Lukas to me.'

'No can do,' Jermaine replied as Edwina, not risking to be caught out if anyone should be lurking unseen, held her 'injured' back with one hand and limped down the stairs with her sister.

'Why not?' Edwina demanded.

'Because I'm here to work this weekend. Lukas has some typing he wants doing.'

'You're staying overnight?'

Jermaine ignored the aggressive question. 'Have you phoned Dad this week?' she asked.

'Don't be a pain!' Edwina retorted, but as she spotted Lukas crossing the hall she was suddenly all smiles. 'Did you know Jermaine was here?' she called down to him.

He halted as they slowly descended. What he was think-ing Jermaine had no idea, for his expression was bland. 'I invited Jermaine to join us,' he replied smoothly.

'Well, you mustn't work her too hard, you naughty man,'

Edwina scolded archly, and as they stepped onto a level with him Jermaine felt her face flame with warm colour. Edwina made it sound every bit as if she had been complaining to her elder sister about being pressed into work.

Jermaine caught his eyes on her and, embarrassed, she looked quickly away. But she fell even more hopelessly in love with Lukas when, suavely, he told Edwina, 'I won't. Though I've a feeling Jermaine would be the last to complain.' And while Jermaine was glowing from that, he asked Edwina solicitously, 'Can you manage as far as the drawing room? Mrs Dobson will bring in some coffee presently.'

Edwina, taking a hold of his arm and leaning against him, swiftly put paid to any remaining glow Jermaine had been feeling. Spiteful darts of jealousy bombarded her and she couldn't bear to watch.

'I'll get the coffee,' she announced as evenly as she could. 'I wanted to go and say hello to Mrs Dobson, anyhow.'

With that she turned and made for the kitchen, acknowledging that her newly discovered love for Lukas had not come alone. It brought with it a whole gamut of other, unsuspected emotions. She who had never hated anyone in her life had hated Lukas on occasion when she had first met him. Oh, how could she ever have hated him? Was it all part and parcel of falling in love? She felt confused suddenly that she didn't know anything. Though she corrected that. The one thing she did know for sure was that there was nothing whatsoever the matter with Edwina.

'I'm here again, Mrs Dobson.' Jermaine found a smile as she entered the kitchen.

While the housekeeper seemed genuinely pleased to see her again and introduced Tina, who had been busy with a coffee pot, Jermaine spotted that a tray had been laid with two cups and saucers.

'May I have an extra cup?' she asked, and passed a pleasant few minutes in conversation with the housekeeper and her helper. Then, insisting she would take the tray, Jermaine carried it to the drawing room.

The extra cup and saucer was not going to be necessary, she discovered. Lukas was there, but got to his feet as she went into the room. 'If you'll excuse me,' he addressed both his female guests, 'I need to go and look at some fencing.'

'He's never still,' Edwina complained the moment he had gone.

'Poor you,' Jermaine replied, and found another unsuspected trait when, having enjoyed Lukas's company last night, she quite enjoyed saying, 'Just now must have been the first time you've seen him since he went to Sweden on Thursday.'

It was not a very nice trait, she knew. But she got paid back for it in full when Edwina, favouring her with a short look, stated, 'I had a very late night last night. In fact, I was still up when Lukas came home.' Jolted, Jermaine instantly visualised her beautiful sister draped prettily on one of the sofas, waiting to go into action the moment Lukas walked in through the door. 'He rang me from Sweden to ask how I was getting along.' Edwina put her delicate size five boot in.

Somehow Jermaine managed to stay civilly in the same room with her while they shared a pot of coffee and spoke of nothing in particular. She should have known, Jermaine inwardly sighed; Edwina always won.

With pictures flashing through her head of Lukas rushing home after he had left her, so that he could dally with her sister, Jermaine finished her coffee and returned the tray to the kitchen. What she would have liked to do then was to escape via the rear door and take a walk down to the picturesque brook. It was such a tranquil spot—and she needed a tranquil spot. She was, in truth, feeling anything but tranquil.

But Lukas was in the grounds somewhere, checking out fences. And, when not long ago she had left her room in a hurry to join him, to spend some time with him, she was now not ready to see him again so soon—should his fence inspection area be anywhere near that brook.

Jermaine, aware that her sister wouldn't be bothered whether she went back to her in the drawing room or not, went upstairs to her room. She would have to go down again for lunch, politeness alone decreed that, but she would by far much prefer to return to London.

But that was a lie. Falling in love with Lukas had made a liar of her—a liar to herself. Because, had she felt that strongly about returning to London, nothing would have stopped her. As it was, despite being in a state of turmoil—not knowing if Lukas, needing a report typing, had deliberately set out to entertain, to charm last night, even to the extent of that oh so wonderful kiss, in order to ask her to come to Highfield today—Jermaine knew she wanted to stay.

She was being weak, not to say pathetic, but she loved him so that even if he was being a rat of the first water she wanted to stay in his home, where she stood the best chance of spending some time with him.

With the passing of the next fifteen minutes Jermaine started to get on top of her emotions, and was then able to think more logically. Come on, buck your ideas up, she instructed. Do you really believe that a man of Lukas's standing, a man of his undoubted wealth, would—*before* he went to Sweden, mark you—arrange to take you out so that on his return he could persuade you, deviously, to come and do some work for him?

Jermaine realised she didn't believe any such nonsense. If he needed someone to work over the weekend, he'd hire somebody. The same way in which he must have instructed Mrs Dobson to hire any help she needed while there were extra people in the house. Clearly Mrs Dobson must have accepted that she couldn't cope without weekend assistance, and had contacted Sharon's sister in Lukas's absence.

Jermaine was still in her room when, glancing from her window, she saw Ash's car turn in at the gates. It puzzled her why if, as he'd hinted, he was not so enamoured of Edwina, he was still harbouring her as his guest. A whole week had passed since he'd stated that he had made a mistake—so why was Edwina still here—though ultimately as Lukas's guest?

At that point Jermaine realised that jealousy in relation to Lukas and Edwina was starting to get to her again, and she was impatient with herself. For goodness' sake, she could hardly expect either Lukas or Ash to send Edwina on her way—not when she was playing the suffering delicate damsel.

Jermaine left her room and, on entering the drawing room, felt jealousy nip again, because Lukas was back from his fence checking and was seated in conversation with Edwina. He broke off what he was saying and was on his feet as soon as he saw her. 'Jermaine,' he greeted her pleasantly. 'Can I get you something to drink before lunch?'

'No, thanks,' she replied, her thoughts on the work for which she would need to keep her full attention focused that afternoon.

She was half turned when someone else came into the drawing room. 'Jermaine!' Ash exclaimed, and again looked as though he might kiss her in greeting. Perhaps remembering the last time he'd tried it, he controlled himself, but still looked delighted to see her as he added, 'This is a wonderful surprise! You're not dashing back to London, I hope?'

'I'm here until tomorrow,' she answered. But, feeling a little awkward, and as if needing an excuse for being there, she explained, 'Lukas has a report on his Swedish trip he wants typing.'

Ash looked from her to his brother. 'Has he now?' he questioned.

'Since we're all here, we may as well go into lunch,' Lukas suggested, and it was *prima donna* time as Edwina winced and nibbled prettily at her bottom lip as she struggled painfully to stand. Naturally, gentlemen both, the two males went to assist her.

The two men seemed a little preoccupied over lunch, but Edwina was obviously insensitive to the vibes Jermaine was certain she was picking up. Edwina kept up a steady flow of conversation to which, when addressed, everyone present politely replied.

It was near to the end of the meal when Ash commented that he thought he would go and take a second look at a property he had almost made up his mind to purchase. Before being asked, Edwina declined. 'You won't mind if I don't come with you?'

Ash smiled. 'You must rest as much as you can,' he answered. Then he turned to Jermaine, seated next to him. 'And you're about to tell me you're going to be busy,' he commented regretfully.

But before she could agree that she would be busy, in his brother's study, Lukas was stating quietly, 'I'll come with you, Ash.' And all eyes went to Lukas. But it was Jermaine to whom he looked as he stated charmingly, 'With the speed you type, Jermaine, we'll have ample time to complete that report tomorrow morning.'

She had straight away decided that if there was nothing there for her to do, then she was here under false pretences—double false pretences if you took into account the charade Edwina was playing to the full—and that she would go back to London right now. But Lukas stating they would work in the morning gave her pride the fillip it needed—he still expected her to stay overnight, then? 'Of course,' she answered evenly.

'You could come with us this afternoon,' Ash suggested.

But somehow she sensed—and could only suppose her senses were more acute to Lukas now than they had been—that he wanted to talk privately to Ash. Something to do with business, obviously, so she smiled, unoffended, and entered her sister's charade. 'I think it would be better if I stayed and kept Edwina company,' she replied.

The two Tavinor brothers departed soon after lunch, and with Edwina comfortable back in the drawing room, with a seemingly limitless supply of magazines, Jermaine went and found the portable telephone she had used on her previous visit. She rang her parents and chatted to them for some while. After confirming that she wouldn't dream of spending Christmas anywhere but with them, in their home, she handed the phone to her sister. Edwina stuck out her tongue to her, but took the phone and assured her father that she was making excellent progress and that she would be leaving Highfield shortly. No, she quickly answered their father, there was absolutely no need for her to go home to be looked after.

Jermaine heard her promise that—as was usual and expected—she also would be home for Christmas. But only one sentence stuck in Jermaine's mind as Edwina ended the call and idly handed the phone back to her. 'You're leaving here?' she questioned.

'Even I can't keep up the pretence of a bad back for ever,' Edwina answered. 'Although were it not for Lukas going away on Monday I'd have given it a shot.'

'You're leaving because Lukas is going abroad?'

'You know as well as I do that he's the only reason for my "incapacity". I'm not sticking around here all next week with only Ash and that odious Mrs Dobson for company!'

Mrs Dobson, odious! Jermaine gave up. 'Got everything you need?' she asked a touch sarcastically as, taking the portable phone with her, she headed for the door.

'No,' Edwina replied, a calculating look there in her eyes, 'but I will have.'

Jermaine blanched and felt quite ill. She'd seen that look in Edwina's eyes before. When Edwina set her mind on something, she always got it—and Edwina was set on getting Lukas.

Jermaine stayed in her room until close to dinner time, when she felt it would be rude to stay there any longer. She had no idea where the property was that Lukas and Ash had gone to see, but they had been absent an absolute age. Jermaine knew, because she had had her ears tuned for every passing vehicle, they had returned a little over half an hour ago.

Dinner was a pleasant enough affair, but Jermaine found she was having a hard time trying not to be forever glancing across to Lukas. Determined not to focus all her attention on him—she'd just shrivel up and die if he observed that she hung on his every word—she turned to Ash.

'Have you decided about the property you saw this afternoon?' she asked.

Ash looked at her and smiled. 'I have. I'm going to make an offer for it.'

'You'll be pleased your long search is at an end.'

'You must come and see it,' Ash invited enthusiastically, but paused, glanced quickly to Lukas, and then looked at Edwina, seated across from him. 'You, too, Edwina. If you feel up to it, of course,' he qualified.

'I'd like to,' she accepted, but, as Jermaine knew full well, Edwina was quite able to find an excuse not to go when the time came. Now, having spent enough time on

Ash apparently, Edwina turned the battery of her blue eyes onto Lukas. 'What did you think of the property, Lukas?' she asked in her breathless way. She even touched his arm.

Jermaine concentrated her attention on a roast parsnip—she was finding the vicious assault of jealousy difficult to cope with.

They retired to the drawing room for coffee. 'Would you care for a liqueur?' Jermaine looked up and found Lukas had come to stand near. 'Cointreau? T…?'

'Cointreau would be lovely,' she accepted, her voice suddenly husky. She looked quickly away from him—about the only way she could get herself back together again.

This was dreadful! She'd gone to pieces over him like some lovestruck schoolgirl! Though, recalling the burning pain of jealousy not too long back, this was no schoolgirl crush. Lukas returned with her liqueur, but when he did no more than sit down next to her Jermaine was again left struggling to get herself together.

'Um—what time would you like to start in the morning?' she asked.

'Any time to suit you,' Lukas replied.

'Nine?'

He smiled. 'I think we can be a little more relaxed than that.' His smile became a grin. 'How do you feel about nine-fifteen?'

She loved him—she burst out laughing. 'Nine-fifteen it is,' she said.

And stopped laughing when Edwina, not caring very much to be sharing her sofa with Ash, suddenly pouted. 'Are you going to share the joke?'

Jermaine realised then that she was laughing too freely with Lukas and might be in danger of giving away her feelings for him. She wanted to stay with him, to be near him, close like this on the sofa. Against that, though, she knew her pride would never recover if he, or anyone in the room, saw the love which she was so desperate to hide. She felt panicky suddenly, and needed to be on her own. She shouldn't have accepted that will-weakening liqueur. Not that she'd done more than have a sip or two, but she needed to be alert, on her toes—needed to be out of there.

Because she'd asked for the Cointreau, she finished it while Edwina, giving Lukas her undivided attention, pulled out all the stops in the allure department. When jealousy again sent fast and furious spiteful darts, Jermaine knew it was more than high time she made herself scarce. It was even more painful to her that Lukas didn't appear at all unhappy that Edwina was dedicated to his every utterance. Surely he must be aware that Edwina was making a play for him? Perhaps he was—and was enjoying every moment.

Jermaine yawned delicately. It wouldn't hurt him to know that such goings-on bored her totally. 'I'm sorry,' she apologised prettily. 'Would anyone mind if I went to bed?'

'Must you?' It was Ash—how she wanted it to be Lukas.

'I've had a busy week.' She smiled at Ash.

'And it isn't over yet,' Lukas said, getting to his feet with her.

'Nine-fifteen, you said,' she reminded him, wished everyone goodnight, and went without obvious haste from the room.

She lay sleepless for a long time that night, then had sleep of the fractured variety and wanted quite urgently to get up and leave. Yet, at the same time, she began to feel quite desperate—because when she did leave she might never see Lukas again.

Jermaine was glad to see dawn break, and, still in the same troubled frame of mind, showered and got dressed. She felt restless and fidgety, and, unable to take it any longer, she shrugged into her coat and decided to take a walk.

Letting herself quietly out of the house, she skirted round

to the rear. Supposing that she had known in advance where her feet would lead her, she was very soon walking down to the bridge with its little stream gurgling cheerfully beneath.

She stayed on the bridge for some minutes, then moved to the bench that seemed to call a welcome. It *was* a tranquil place, as she had previously discovered, and gradually Jermaine became more at peace with herself. She was then able to recognise that, probably because she had never been in love before, she had been thrown in a total heap by it and just hadn't known how to handle it.

She still didn't know how to handle it, particularly, but this morning she seemed more reconciled to the fact that, while she loved Lukas, he was never going to return that love—and so she had better get used to that foul companion, jealousy, whenever any female flirted with him.

Jermaine was just wryly musing that since she was unlikely to see him again after today there was nothing to get used to, when she was suddenly shaken to realise that she had company of a very special kind.

'Couldn't you sleep?'

She looked up, a smile in her heart, in her eyes, as she stared at Lukas. 'Early to bed, early to rise,' she trotted out.

'Shall I join you?' he asked.

'Of course,' she replied, and, on a sudden thought, 'I didn't disturb you when I left the house, did I?' she asked hurriedly.

He shook his head. 'I was in my study when I heard dainty footsteps going over the gravel on the drive,' he answered. 'Now, how did I know I'd find you down here?'

'I'm bewitched by this spot,' she smiled, but, her head jerking up, 'You—followed me?' she asked, her already hurried heartbeat picking up more speed at the notion before common sense landed. 'You wanted me for something?' she dully realised. 'You wanted to have a word about…?'

'I need to have a reason?' Lukas teased—and her heart fluttered again.

'Er—no,' she replied, telling herself she mustn't take any of this personally. 'They're your grounds, after all.'

Lukas didn't answer. He didn't move away either, but seemed perfectly content at that hour in the morning to sit quietly with her, watching the clear waters of the dancing brook as it leapt over pebbles.

Then suddenly, astonishingly, she heard him say, 'So who's this man you've got to rush back to London to see tonight?'

'Sorry?' she queried blankly, staring at him mystified.

'You said you couldn't stay until Monday morning,' Lukas reminded her—she didn't remember saying any such thing. 'When I asked you to stay the weekend, you said you needed to be back in London for Sunday evening.' Now she remembered—she hadn't wanted to appear too eager. 'Is it the diabolical Stuart that takes you away from us?' Lukas wanted to know.

She laughed. She didn't want to laugh. She had an idea that just being with him made her so happy that laughter just kind of bubbled up inside her. Still, all the same, she didn't feel like telling Lukas that she had absolutely no need whatsoever to dash back to London that afternoon. At the very least he would think it odd that she had said she had to in the first place. She saw his glance move from her violet eyes to her laughing mouth, and she reined in her inner happiness to tell him primly, 'Stuart isn't diabolical. He's…'

'You're not in love with him, I know that much,' Lukas cut in.

How did he know? She panicked for a moment, until she recalled Lukas saying on Friday that he didn't see her as someone who'd be serious with one man and be out dining with another. 'I don't need to be in love with him,' she replied, and, in the manner of some newsworthy film star, she ended, 'We're just good friends.' She started to feel a mite anxious that with this mention of love Lukas might probe deeper—though why he would was ridiculous—and stood up. 'I've an appointment at nine-fifteen,' she mentioned lightly. 'I shall have to go.'

Lukas gave her an amused look, but left the bench too. Together they walked back to the house, each occupied with their own thoughts. They parted at the stairs with little else being said, apart from Lukas commenting, 'If I miss you at breakfast, I'll see you in the study.'

Jermaine went up to her room with her insides all wobbly—partly from her unexpected meeting with Lukas, and partly from her anticipation of shortly seeing him again.

She delayed going down to breakfast for as long as she could, and discovered from Ash that Lukas had breakfasted some while ago. 'So you're stuck with just me,' he smiled, and was so exceedingly pleasant and likeable that Jermaine realised that, had circumstances been different, they could have been very good friends.

'Must dash,' she said when she had finished the bacon and scrambled eggs Tina had brought her.

'Don't let that brother of mine work you too hard.' Ash smiled.

Jermaine returned briefly to her room to wash her hands, clean her teeth and to check that she was looking all right. Her platinum-blonde hair was shining and needed little attention. Likewise her make-up required little attention. It was her insides that she could do nothing about.

She wanted to see him. She so wanted to see him. So what are you doing, dithering up here? It had never been her habit to wait until the clock struck nine to start work.

If she arrived at the office early she began work straight away.

At five past nine, passing Tina in the hall carrying a tray, obviously on her way to Edwina's room, Jermaine made it to the study door. She took a steadying breath and went in, her heart performing a jig when she at once saw that Lukas was there first.

'Oh, good,' she smiled. 'You're here.'

'Here and waiting,' Lukas answered quietly, his serious grey eyes taking in her shoulder-length hair, her superb complexion and her slender but shapely figure. 'Come in and sit down,' he said when she hadn't moved, and smiled.

Jermaine hung the jacket of her suit over the chair she had used before—and in no time they were deep into his work concerning Sweden.

It could, she supposed, have been some deadly boring business report. But, possibly because of her own business background, and because of the overwhelming love she felt for him, Jermaine thought his report little short of terrific.

'Shall we take a break?' Lukas asked at one stage. But suddenly she felt strangely shy.

She shook her head. 'Shall we get on?' She made the mistake of looking at him, and at the warm look in his eyes for her her pulses raced.

'A woman after my own heart,' he said softly, and while Jermaine wanted to tell him, yes, yes, she wanted his heart, he continued from where they had left off.

It was nearing half past twelve when everything was neatly typed and many copies printed and checked over. Jermaine felt Lukas come and stand behind her.

'You've worked like a Trojan,' he commented, and she looked up, awash with pleasure.

'I enjoyed doing it,' she answered truthfully, turning and basking in the warm look in his eyes. They stared at each other, and she felt transfixed to look away. Her heart started drumming and there was a pounding in her ears too. But abruptly she stood up. 'I'd b-better go and tidy up before lunch,' she mumbled huskily, desperately trying to get herself together; with Lukas looking steadily at her like that— a certain indefinable warmth in his eyes—something, she knew not what, was happening to her, and she urgently needed to find some sort of control.

She went to shoot past him, failed to clear him, violently bumped into him, and they ended up facing each other. His hands came to her arms as he steadied her. 'Now what are you panicking over?' Lukas asked, not letting her go.

'N-nothing,' she said. 'I'm not...'

'You're afraid I'm going to kiss you?'

Please, oh, please do. 'Of course not!' she answered, her voice coming out nowhere near as firm as she would have liked to have heard it.

A frown crossed his intelligent forehead. 'You're not scared of me, Jermaine?' he asked quietly—and suddenly she was remembering how he had gently probed 'You're scared' when he had learned she was a virgin.

Because she loved him, and had all at once realised that he had a fine sensitivity, she was not thinking but just acting on instinct alone. Jermaine showed him in the only way she could that she was not scared, or afraid he would kiss her. She stretched up, and she kissed him...

Then found she didn't want to break away. Her hands went to his waist—just the feel of his excellent mouth against her own and she seemed to need to steady herself.

She quickly pulled back; that, or kiss him again. 'I— er—um—shouldn't have done that,' she said huskily, and loved it when, slowly, Lukas smiled.

'Oh, I can't agree with you there,' he murmured, and, taking charge, he pulled her into his arms. The next she knew he was kissing her as she had never been kissed before.

Nor did he stop at one kiss; he seemed as hungry for her mouth as she was for his. Locked in his warm embrace, Jermaine welcomed his kisses, a fire igniting in her, bursting into flame as his strong arms held her, binding her to him.

'Beautiful, beautiful Jermaine,' he breathed against her mouth, kissing her again, gathering her yet closer to him.

She felt his warmth, his heat, and as he pressed close to her, she, her heart going crazy, pressed closer to him. She heard a groan of wanting escape him, and felt she would faint from the utter rapture of it when, with his mouth on hers, drawing her very soul from her, his caressing hands sought and found the swollen globes of her breasts.

She wasn't sure that a groan of wanting didn't escape her too, for Lukas broke his kiss to smile tenderly down at her. 'All right?' he asked.

Wonderfully all right, she wanted to tell him. But as the flame of unsuspected passion continued to spiral upward in her, and she found herself in a never-before-known land of urgent desire, of wanting, with no thought of holding back, she could only suppose it must be some latent and totally-not-required strand of modesty that caused her to answer, 'I'm not very sure we should be doing this.'

Those grey eyes were as steady as ever as Lukas looked into her fervent violet ones, that had darkened to a much deeper colour as her desire for him had rocked her. Then she saw his mouth pick up at the corners.

'Why?' he asked gently, teasingly.

Again she recalled his 'scared' comment, and she didn't *want* him to think she was scared of him, or of making love with him, and so she told him honestly, 'Because I—um—think I like it.'

He laughed then, and it was a wonderful sound. 'You're simply gorgeous,' he said softly. But instead of renewing his onslaught to her mouth, to her senses, when he must know the advantage was all his, he kissed her tenderly and, taking his arms from her, took a small step away. 'And absolutely right, of course.'

'I am?' She hoped she didn't sound as disappointed as she felt.

'It's nearly lunchtime—we could be interrupted at any moment,' he reminded her.

'I—see,' she said slowly, and as she did begin to see, and went hot all over as she visualised Tina perhaps coming in to tell them that the meal was ready, Jermaine moved back from him. Ridiculously, when she considered how not long since she had been clinging to Lukas like a second skin, she was suddenly overcome by a dreadful shyness.

She turned desperately away, warm colour rushing to her face, and was glad to espy her jacket—completely forgotten about until then—still hanging over the back of the chair. She grabbed it up and quickly put it on.

'I'll—er—see you later,' she threw in his general direction. But made the mistake of looking at him.

'Don't rush off,' he said, and, coming close again, caused her insides to jump some more when he stroked tender fingers down the shy blush of her cheek and asked, 'What are you doing for Christmas?'

She was mesmerised by him and tried hard to concentrate. What *was* she doing for Christmas? 'I'm spending it with my parents,' she replied, barely able to remember that part of her telephone conversation with her mother yesterday where she had doubly confirmed that she would be there.

'All of it?' Lukas asked.

'All of it,' she answered, her head swimming as she tried to decipher what all this was about.

'Can I come too?' he asked.

She knew then that he was joking! A man of his charm, his sophistication, would have something better to do than spend a homey Christmas with her and her parents. 'What?' she questioned, pretending to be aghast. 'And let your fan club down?' Jermaine was certain, Edwina aside, that his festive season engagement diary would be full to overflowing.

He grinned. Then, to her amazement, urged, 'Spend your Christmas here?'

Her heart started to pound. Was he serious? Of course he wasn't. Couldn't be, she decided, and fearing to make an utter fool of herself by allowing herself to take him seriously, insisted, 'My parents are expecting me.'

'You always do what your parents expect?' he asked, humour playing around his superb mouth, and she felt light-hearted suddenly.

Though she kept a straight face as she assured him, 'Always.'

'You'll come home Boxing Day?'

'Home?' She wasn't sure she understood his question.

'Home—here. To Highfield,' Lukas answered.

Oh, how she loved him. She had to look away from him. She wanted to swallow on the knot of emotion that caught in her throat—he *had* been serious. She felt then that she would have given anything to tell Lukas yes, yes, a thousand times yes. By the sound of it all her prayers would be answered and she *would* be able to see Lukas again when he returned from his business trip. But the reality of it was that her parents would be very much upset, and hurt, if she and Edwina broke their promise to spend Christmas with them.

So, from somewhere, Jermaine managed to summon up a smile, and, much though it hurt her, 'I can't,' she told Lukas. 'I gave them my promise.'

CHAPTER SEVEN

THE days stretched long and achingly for Jermaine after her departure from Highfield. She had not managed to have a moment alone with Lukas once she had left his study— Edwina had seemed to be always everywhere.

Jermaine spent hours reliving those minutes she had been in his arms. She again felt the rapture of being held by him and of being kissed by him.

He had been in no hurry for her to leave, she recalled dreamily, and felt warmed through and through to remember, again and again, that Lukas had asked her to spend Christmas with him at Highfield. Ash would be there too, of course, but surely Lukas wouldn't have asked her to Christmas at Highfield on any mere passing whim?

To invite someone into your home over that special festive time had to mean that they were a tiny bit special too, didn't it?

Oh, come off it, argued her more realistic self. You're not even the tiniest scrap special to him. Have you forgotten so completely that he regards you as a bit of a challenge? Good heavens, get your head together do. For pity's sake, you don't have to look further back than Sunday, when *you* kissed *him*. You responded fully when he kissed you back; my, how you responded! Lukas must have thought, No challenge; a walk-over! And *that* was why he invited you to spend Christmas in his home, purely and simply because he thought you were *willing!*

Well, she wasn't willing—well, that was what she tried to tell herself. Although, as she recalled just how eager she

118

had been for his kisses, in all honesty she couldn't have said that she was *un*willing.

Pride insisted on reminding her that she had demurred a little when she'd told him that she wasn't very sure they should be doing this. But only for her pride to take a hammering when she recollected how he'd agreed a very short while afterwards that she was absolutely right.

Perhaps, then, that meant that he'd decided she was not so much as 'a bit' of a challenge after all. Then why had he asked her to spend Christmas in his home?

At that point Jermaine realised she had come full circle. That did not stop her from thinking continually about Lukas. But she had never been in love before. Though as she did not want to listen to her common sense, her realism, as a few days passed, so she had to accept that she was not the remotest bit special to Lukas. Had she been, then surely he would have managed to pick up the phone—wherever he was? When he'd been in Sweden he'd found a moment to ring Edwina, Jermaine recalled.

No, no, no, she was not going to think of Edwina in relation to Lukas. She couldn't, Jermaine fretted. There were enough emotions tearing at her nerves now, without adding jealousy.

She had never felt so low, but, since she was the only one who was going to know it, Jermaine adopted a cheerfulness she was far from feeling. The evening of the company's Christmas dinner came—with Nick Norris eager to take her home.

'I'm driving Stuart home,' she was glad to be able to answer.

'You mean I have to wait until the New Year to get to spend any time with you?' he complained. But, brightening, he persisted, 'Fancy partnering me at a New Year's Eve party?'

She didn't. 'Some other time,' she told him, and tried to feel good that somebody wanted to date her anyhow.

She went out for an Indian meal with Stuart on Friday, was home by ten, and spent the weekend half wishing she had been able to break her promise to her parents and go to Highfield for Christmas instead. Even while she hated herself for that half wish, Jermaine couldn't help but fully wish she had been in a position to accept Lukas's Christmas offer. She ached to see Lukas again, wanted to see him again—oh, so desperately.

Jermaine spent her lunchtimes on Monday and Tuesday doing her last bits of Christmas shopping, and went home to her parents on Christmas Eve, laden with a large suitcase plus many carrier bags, where she was warmly welcomed—and, metaphorically, dropped from a great height when, greetings over, she asked what time Edwina was expected.

'She's not coming,' Grace Hargreaves replied flatly.

'Not...?'

'They so badly wanted her to stay, it seemed criminal to keep her to her promise,' Edwin Hargreaves defended. 'Especially as Edwina has been through such a rough time with her back.'

'They?' Jermaine asked, fearing the worst but striving to keep her expression even, as looking to her father, she waited for him to deliver the body-blow.

'The Tavinors, of course!' her father replied. 'Edwina rang this afternoon and was quite excited that Lukas Tavinor himself had just been in touch, asking her to join him and Ash. Having met them both, I'm happy that they'll take care of her—I told her to go, with my blessing. She's not fully recovered yet, you know.'

Jermaine was aware that her father was defending in advance any criticism of his elder daughter's actions, but Jermaine was too heartsick to think of telling him that Edwina was more than capable of taking care of herself.

As the evening progressed it became apparent, when the subject of Edwina frequently came up, that her father was of the opinion that it was only because Lukas Tavinor was head of the household that he had personally phoned Edwina to ask her to stay. However, in Edwin Hargreaves's view, it was really his brother Ash who had extended the invitation.

Oh, how Jermaine would have loved to have believed that. But she knew differently. Hadn't Ash himself told her he'd made one colossal mistake where Edwina was concerned, and had allowed lust to rule his head? From that Jermaine could only imagine Ash meant that Edwina was now out of his system. It therefore figured that it wasn't Ash who wanted Edwina at Highfield over Christmas—but Lukas.

Inconstant swine! Inconstant? Just because he asked you first? For heaven's sake. Jermaine brought herself up short. Anyone would think Lukas had declared undying love to her, when all he'd done was to ask her to spend Christmas with him and, when she'd refused, asked her sister instead. Well, wasn't that inconstant? No, it wasn't. What it was was telling her that she might refuse his invitation but that there were dozens of others who would accept. Indeed, someone already had. Someone ready and more than willing to drop her other plans and dash to Highfield.

Christmas Day passed with an exchange of gifts and Jermaine helping with the preparation for the evening meal. Needing a break from being forever cheerful, she took herself off for a long walk during the afternoon.

She discovered on her return that her father had been unable to wait any longer for Edwina to ring, as he'd expected, and that he'd telephoned Highfield himself. Jermaine was glad she had not been there. Her father might well have asked her to get him the Highfield number, and she didn't know, should Lukas have answered the phone, whether or not she would have wanted to speak to him.

Jermaine wasn't sleeping well. That night was no exception. Had Edwina been in Lukas's study? Had he kissed her the way he'd kissed...? Jermaine blanked off her mind, but was still wide awake, sitting up in the window seat in her room, at one o'clock on Boxing Day morning, when it began to snow.

She watched for some while as huge flakes quickly covered the ground. How silent everywhere was, how beautiful the night. She wished she were with Lukas. Pathetic. She sighed and got into bed. Put the man out of your mind, do.

But he was even more difficult to put out of her mind when later, around eleven that morning, when she had just hunted out some old snow boots with a view to taking herself off for another solitary walk, Jermaine, shrugging into a jacket, heard the sound of a vehicle crunching over the snow-covered drive.

'Who's this?' she heard her mother ask, plainly not recognising the vehicle as belonging to any of their friends.

Jermaine went and joined her, and, taking a glance out of the window, saw a Range Rover standing there. When none other than Lukas Tavinor stepped out of it, she thought—as a symphony started up in her head—that she'd had him so much on her mind her brain had conjured him up; that because she so wanted to see him she was imagining it was him.

But Lukas was no figment of her imagination. 'Isn't he Lukas, Ash's brother?' her mother exclaimed. As Grace Hargreaves worriedly pondered, 'Do you think something's happened to Edwina?' Jermaine had to try to rapidly get herself together.

'I shouldn't think so for a minute,' she answered, glad her father was out at the village shop, hunting up some reading matter. He'd panic like crazy if he thought Edwina had had 'another' accident.

The doorbell sounded and Jermaine, who would by far have preferred her mother to answer it while she composed herself a little more, went to the door. If something awful *had* befallen Edwina, and Lukas was coming to tell them in person rather than break bad news over the phone, then Jermaine saw it was up to her to answer the door.

A blast of cold air hit her as she pulled back the door—she barely noticed it.

Oh, how wonderful it was to see him. Her heart felt so full that for long, long seconds time seemed suspended and she just stared at him.

Lukas too seemed stuck for words as he looked back at her, though she very soon realised her imagination was going off at a tangent. For, as casually as you like, he was suddenly saying, 'I was in the area...' And with a smile that turned her knees to water, he continued, 'I thought I might stop by and cadge a cup of coffee.'

The sun came out on the whole miserable time she'd had since she had last seen him. A smile started deep inside her. 'I was just going out for a walk,' she blurted out—and could have kicked herself. Now she'd just deprived herself of fifteen minutes, perhaps half an hour, of his company.

'You're going on your own?' he enquired.

'I love the snow,' she said, and wondered what was happening to her brain. That was no sort of an answer.

'No diabolical Stuart walking with you?'

She laughed. Oh, joy, oh, bliss, just to see Lukas. 'Everything all right?' Her mother appearing at her shoulder brought Jermaine abruptly down to earth. All too plainly there was nothing the matter with Edwina, and her mother should be told so at once.

Jermaine opened her mouth to tell her that Lukas had merely stopped by for a cup of coffee when, to Jermaine's delight, he said, 'Good morning, Mrs Hargreaves. I've come to borrow your lovely daughter for a walk, if you've no objection.'

Grace Hargreaves was all smiles, and, to Jermaine's total embarrassment, she obviously believed Lukas had driven the many miles on such a bad-weather day merely to take her youngest daughter for a walk. But, before Jermaine could find her voice and say that Lukas just happened to be in the area, her mother was inviting, 'Perhaps you'd like to stay to lunch when you come back? After yesterday's feasting we're only having a cold meal today, but you're more than welcome.'

'Thank you,' he promptly accepted, and Jermaine forgot everything, save that she had just been assured of a couple of hours, or more, of Lukas's company.

'See you later,' she said to her mother.

Buttoning up her jacket as she went, Jermaine tried desperately hard as Lukas fell into step with her for some kind of normality. 'You've Edwina staying with you, I believe,' she said nicely as they approached some of her father's outbuildings.

'She's having a lie-in this morning,' Lukas replied.

Because she had a late night last night? Jermaine wondered, and, as sudden jealousy raged at that thought, she found she had stepped inside one of the outbuildings—as if to get away from Lukas himself.

'Looking for something?' he enquired, following her in, observing that she appeared to be staring into space.

Oh, heavens! Jermaine abruptly collected herself and knew she would just about die if Lukas gathered so much as an inkling of the savage green-eyed emotion that racked her when she thought of him with her sister.

'There's a sledge in here somewhere,' some guardian angel remembered for her. Jermaine looked at him then,

saw him affable, friendly—and sophisticated. 'But of
course you wouldn't...'

'I would,' he promptly assured her.

She stared at him. 'You wouldn't?'

'Would,' he said.

She laughed, and knew then, even though she might regret it later, that she was going to enjoy this time with him.
She loved him so, and had missed him more than she had
dreamt it was possible to miss anyone.

The sledge, when they found it, was rusty and cobwebby,
but otherwise sound. 'Lead on, Miss Hargreaves,' Lukas
commanded, taking hold of the rope and pulling the sledge
behind him. 'Presumably you know the best sledging
spots.'

'You know you're going to get soaked?'

'I don't care,' he said, and looked so terrifically wonderful that Jermaine wanted quite dreadfully to kiss him.

She looked away and desperately fought to banish any
such impossible impulses, while seeking to find any safe
topic that would get her away from this moment of weak-
ness. 'So, what did Santa bring you for Christmas?' she
asked lightly.

Lukas was silent for a few moments. 'Not what I
wanted,' he answered at length.

'Shame,' she jibed. 'You couldn't have been a very good
boy.'

'That's the trouble,' Lukas complained. 'I've been so
good, you just wouldn't believe.'

'I wouldn't,' she laughed, feeling then that she wanted
to give him a consoling hug, and was glad that they had
arrived at the small trio of hills they'd been making for.

They didn't have the hills to themselves, but for Jermaine
there was no one else there as she gave herself up to the
sublime pleasure of just being with the man she loved. Up
and down the hills they trekked, she squealing, Lukas

laughing, as they bumped and tumbled—and never had she been more happy.

She wasn't feeling hungry, but guessed it must be nearing lunchtime when the assorted bunches of sledgers started to thin out, until there was just her and Lukas there.

Her conscience prodded her. 'We'd better go back.'

But she felt that Lukas was as reluctant as she when he suggested, 'Just one more.'

'Your trouble is you've never grown up,' taunted she to the man whom she full well knew carried a tremendous load of responsibility on his shoulders.

'I'm allowed to play sometimes,' he declared, dramatically and defiantly. She laughed, and she wanted to kiss him again, because he was just so—Lukas—but couldn't.

'Come on, then,' she sighed, equally dramatically. 'Just one more.'

Together they climbed up the hill for the last time and sat close together—and moved off. Gathering speed as they travelled the short trip, Jermaine just knew that this time they were going to come to grief—she didn't care. Never had she enjoyed an outing so much. This time was precious to her, and would live in her memory for ever.

They were going too fast, the route having become icy with use, and they did come to grief; in fact there was no way in which Lukas could prevent it. They both came off the sledge, but as she lay looking at the bluest of skies on a sunny winter's day Jermaine just had to laugh from the pure and utter joy of it.

Then, all at once, something was blotting out the sun. Lukas was leaning over her and looking down at her—and still she laughed. Lukas continued to stare down at her, his eyes warm, and somehow tender.

She saw him swallow, and imagined he liked her quite a lot when he said softly, 'Look at you. Soaked. Your wonderful hair soaked, your make-up long gone. Know something?' he asked, and when she shook her head he told her, 'You look absolutely fantastic.'

Jermaine loved him. She loved him, loved him. 'Is my nose red?' she asked, her mouth still smiling.

He bent and kissed her nose. 'It's like ice,' he stated.

'You should see yours, mister,' she laughed, and he kissed her once more. Suddenly it was the best Christmas she'd ever had. 'I'll give you thirty minutes to pack that up,' she told him cheekily, and a kind of groan escaped him.

Then he was kissing her, and again kissing her, and holding her, and she was kissing and holding him in return. 'I've missed you,' he murmured against her mouth. But she couldn't believe he had said what she wanted him to say—that he'd missed her—so she kissed him.

Lukas looked into her lovely violet eyes as the kiss ended, and then tenderly he kissed her snow-chilled face. 'Come on, let's get you back home. You're frozen,' he declared, helping her to her feet.

Jermaine didn't feel in the least frozen, but supposed she had been too nicely brought up to confess about the fire he had caused to burst into flame within her.

They were silent but companionable on the short walk back to her family home, where her wonderful mother had asked Lukas to stay to lunch. She had about another hour of his company, Jermaine mused, and she was going to enjoy it. That life was going to be pretty bleak afterwards—well, she just wasn't going to think about when Lukas left today.

'I'm sorry if we're a little late,' Lukas apologised to her mother, as they stood in the hall shedding their top clothes.

'There's nothing to spoil,' Grace Hargreaves assured him. 'But you're both soaked!' she scolded, instantly forgiving Lukas his every sin when he smiled.

Jermaine looked across at Lukas to see how this giant in

the world of big business was taking being scolded, and was delighted to see that he appeared to be quite enjoying her mother mothering him.

And mother him she did. While she sent Jermaine upstairs to have a hot shower, Jermaine heard her showing Lukas the downstairs facility, requesting his topcoat and suggesting he let her have his clothes for her to whip round in the tumbledrier.

Jermaine, while wanting to hurry to be back with Lukas, thawed herself out under the hot shower, and then washed her already shampooed-that-day hair. But by the time she had dried her hair and had decided, since he had been dressed casually, that she would dress casually too, she could wait no longer to see him again.

Swiftly, her long legs encased in a smart pair of trousers, Jermaine went down the stairs. She found Lukas and her parents in the drawing room, and saw at once that Lukas must have submitted to her mother's ministrations.

'All dry?' Jermaine commented, more because she felt suddenly shy to have this man in her family home, where it must appear that he was *her* visitor.

Lukas studied her. 'No ill effects?'

'You came off the sledge, naturally,' her father commented before she could reply, and continued, though it was totally untrue, even if he must have believed it to be true, 'Edwina always used to love sledging.'

After that, it seemed as if no other topic could be raised without Edwina's name being brought into the conversation by Edwin Hargreaves. They moved to the dining room to eat, but lunch was not a comfortable meal for Jermaine, and she was beginning to regret that Lukas had ever come or that her mother had invited him to share their meal. Jermaine was used to her father singing Edwina's praises, but Lukas wasn't. Might he not be weary of it?

Jermaine's new-found enemy jealousy suddenly started

an attack; perhaps Lukas wasn't weary of it? He had, after all, invited Edwina into his home for Christmas. In fact in his home was where Edwina was right at this minute.

So what the dickens was Lukas doing here, with her?

Jermaine had come to no sort of conclusion before her father was suddenly embarrassing her to death by saying, very pointedly from where she was viewing it, 'Of course, Edwina's being extremely brave. She hasn't fully recovered from that injury to her back yet.'

'Backs can be the very devil,' Lukas agreed evenly.

'I'm not sure she's fit enough to even now be left on her own—without another female in the house,' Edwin Hargreaves hinted, and Jermaine wasn't sure whether she went ashen, or scarlet.

In the ensuing silence, she wanted the floor to open up and swallow her. She was aware of Lukas's eyes on her, but she wouldn't, couldn't, look at him after her father's very near outright suggestion that Lukas take her back to Highfield with him.

She sought desperately hard for some topic with which to change the conversation, but was so swamped with mortification that she couldn't think straight. Which meant she had to leave it to Lukas or her mother to change the conversation.

Only her mother was saying nothing, and when Lukas did speak, Jermaine was staggered that he didn't change the topic at all, but told her father, 'I did ask Jermaine to spend her Christmas at Highfield, but...'

'You did?' her father cut in, jovial all of a sudden as he turned to glance at his younger daughter.

'I promised you and M...' she began, but was cut off before she could finish.

'You must have known that neither your mother nor I would hold you to that sort of promise if you'd prefer to spend that time with your friends,' her father remarked, and

Jermaine heartily wished she'd got the nerve to run from the room.

Were it not for drawing attention to the fact that inwardly she was dying of embarrassment here, she might very well have made a dash for it. But by no chance was she going to let Lukas know how utterly miserable this whole conversation was making her.

Though, quietly, he was suddenly saying, 'The offer is still there, Jermaine.'

She looked at him then, saw a sensitivity in his fine grey eyes—but didn't want his pity. 'I'm sorry,' she began to decline—only for her father to speak over the top of her.

'There you are,' he cut in cheerfully. 'Here's Lukas, pleased to have you stay. You'll be able to check if Edwina is all right when she says she's all right, and not just putting a brave face on it, and...'

'It's very kind of Lukas,' Jermaine interrupted, starting to feel desperate, 'but I couldn't possibly...'

'Of course you can,' her father triumphed. 'You're not going back to work until January the second, so...'

'I can't!' Ye gods, her father would have her spend the next seven nights at Highfield, when she was sure Lukas had only meant his invitation for one or two!

'You can, you know,' Lukas said softly, by her side. And, when she stared unhappily at him, he added, 'I'd very much like you to.'

Her heart did a crazy kind of flip—he sounded, looked, so sincere. 'That's settled, then,' Edwin Hargreaves announced.

Jermaine looked from Lukas to her father, and then to her mother, who appeared for once as if she might want to bury an axe in her husband's head, but was too polite to start one of her rare altercations with him in company.

'What do you want to do, sweetheart?' Mrs Hargreaves dared her husband's wrath by asking her younger daughter.

But when Jermaine, because the feeling of humiliation was weighing her down, was about to tell her mother that she didn't want to go anywhere, Lukas was lightly organising, 'We'll go in my vehicle—I don't want you having trouble driving your car if we're snowed in at Highfield.'

She hadn't thought as far as that. 'My car?' she questioned witlessly, while thinking she really should stir herself, even if she was unused to opposing her father.

'I'll bring you back to collect it,' Lukas assured her, as if that was what he thought her question was all about. And when she looked at him, he smiled his devastating smile and added, 'You'd better bring your overnight bag.'

By the time Jermaine had packed her case and was ready to go back down the stairs again, some of her mighty bewilderment was starting to clear. It was then that, while knowing her father would make the rest of her holiday quite awful if she told him she wasn't going to Highfield and her sister, Jermaine also knew that, while she couldn't possibly stay on in her old home, neither could she go to Highfield with Lukas.

'Ready?' Lukas asked when he saw her, taking her case from her and, with her father, going out to the Range Rover.

Jermaine turned to her mother. 'Bye, Mum,' she said, giving her a hug and a kiss.

But her mother didn't let her go. 'Are you all right about this, love?' she asked, going on, 'I saw you and Lukas coming back from sledging—and you looked so happy to be with him. But if you're not, and you don't want to go, you must stay—and I'll deal with your bullying father.'

What could she say? To agree that she felt bullied and browbeaten by her father would only cause disharmony in the home, and who wanted that kind of atmosphere at Christmas?

'Do you mind—about my going? About me breaking my promise?' was what she did answer, and her mother smiled.

'Much as I would want to, I always knew I couldn't keep you with me for ever.'

Jermaine went out to the four-wheel drive feeling very much cheered. They weren't a family who went in for saying how much they loved each other. But, from what her mother had just said, Jermaine knew, as she supposed she'd always known, that as her father idolised his elder daughter, her mother loved her younger daughter very much.

Though that did nothing to alter the fact that Jermaine had decided she was going to spend the rest of her Christmas in her own small flat. Which was why when, having said goodbye to her parents and Lukas having driven a mile down the road, Jermaine asked if he would mind driving to a nearby taxi rank and stopping to let her out.

He did not wait until then to stop, but pulled over at once and turned to look at her. 'Aren't we having fun any more?' he asked, his grey eyes steady on her serious face.

Her heart turned over at the gentleness in his expression. But while it warmed her through and through that Lukas seemed to be saying that he'd enjoyed their time in the snow together every bit as much as she, it just wouldn't do.

'I can't come with you,' she blurted out in a rush.

'What did I do?' he teased gently.

'You—didn't do anything.'

'What did I say?' he persisted. 'That makes you want to deprive me of your company?'

Deprive? Her intention faltered—but pride wasn't so easily defeated. 'You didn't say anything,' she answered honestly. 'But you know as well as I that until less than an hour ago you'd no intention of taking me back to Highfield with you. I can't come with you,' she repeated, feeling quite wretched.

'Even if I want you to?' he smiled coaxingly.

Oh, don't, Lukas! Her pride seemed to be a very wishy-washy thing. Again she hauled it back to attention. 'If my father...' she began, and halted, torn by loyalty not to bring her parent into this. But, since all this was of her father's making, she was unable to see how she could avoid doing so.

Lukas came in and helped her out. 'My dear, Jermaine,' he turned her bones to water by saying quietly, 'believe me, I want very much that you should come and stay at Highfield.'

'But...' she tried to insist, her brain a poor organ in the light of Lukas stating he wanted *very much* that she should stay at Highfield.

'And,' he went on, when she seemed a little stuck, 'if your father, in his concern over Edwina, hadn't suggested it, I would have.'

Jermaine stared at Lukas, wanting quite desperately to believe him. Would he have—or was he just saying that to soothe her wounded pride? 'You would have?' she asked slowly. With those steady grey eyes of his fixed on her and his 'my dear Jermaine' still dancing dreamily about in her head, she didn't seem capable of better argument than that.

'I would have,' he confirmed, and, smiling a gentle smile, he leaned to her and tenderly, without haste, he kissed her. Then, still unhurriedly, he pulled back and looked into her warm violet eyes. 'You'll come—to please me?' he asked softly.

Oh, yes, yes! urged everything in her. 'If—you're sure,' she answered huskily.

'I've never been more sure of anything,' Lukas murmured, and looked deeply into her eyes for long, long moments, 'Trust me?' he asked, and seemed unwilling to look away. It even seemed, Jermaine felt in a bemused kind of way, as if he had to force himself to turn the key in the ignition and to drive on.

Never had she ever felt such a fluttery mess of jumbled emotions that she didn't know where to start first in order to sort herself out. Lukas had called her 'my dear' and had sounded as if he meant it. Somehow she had an idea he was a man who was never too free with his endearments. He had said that he wanted her in his home; her—not Edwina—but *her*.

Jermaine was silent beside him as he steered the Range Rover in the direction of Highfield. Her every instinct seemed to be telling her, screaming at her, that it was her that Lukas wanted, regardless of Edwina being already established in his home—her, not her sister.

Never had Jermaine felt so full of love for him, so excited and yet, at the same time, apprehensive too. She didn't know if she should believe that there was anything more to his invitation than was on the surface. Didn't know if she dared to let herself believe that there might be. But Lukas needn't have called to see her while he was in the area that morning, need he? But he had. *And,* he'd said he would have asked her to come back to Highfield with him—without her father's massive hint.

Jermaine felt so shaky inside it would not have surprised her at all if she were not thinking straight. But, and she had probably got it crazily wrong, but dared she imagine that Lukas had come over specially to see her?

At that point she realised that the events of that day—Lukas turning up out of the blue, their fun together in the snow—had addled her brain.

What was irrefutable, however—while she sat beside Lukas, her insides still a nonsense—was that she was going to his home with him. She, who had been down in the depths that she might never see him again was going to his home with him and would stay overnight there. Oh, weren't the fates just too, too splendid? Not only was she seeing him now, right at this very minute, but she would see him again tomorrow too. What better Christmas could anyone in love have?

She turned her head to look at him just as Lukas turned to look at her. 'Happy?' he asked.

She was too full to speak. She nodded, and then smiled. He had asked her to trust him—and trust him she did.

being with him had would not have minded if he ... ... to ... ... those that her, nor minded? Not only was she beside him now, ... day ... ... but she didn't see him again tomorrow ... ... there'd be ... ... to love ... ...

CHAPTER EIGHT

BOTH Ash and Edwina came out on to the drive when they saw Lukas's vehicle pull up. But they did not stand close together, in fact were some yards apart, and Jermaine received a very clear impression that they were no longer at all friendly.

Ash came round to the passenger door immediately he saw her. 'Jermaine! What a lovely surprise!' he exclaimed, yet didn't seem at all surprised to see Lukas take her case from the vehicle.

Jermaine had not seen Lukas greet her sister, and, as the teeth of jealousy gave her a spiteful nip, she was glad she'd missed any too friendly greeting that might cause more green-eyed darts to bombard her.

Edwina smiled a pretty smile as Jermaine approached her, but Jermaine didn't miss the hardness in her sister's eyes as, still smiling prettily, she hissed, 'What the devil's going on?'

'How's your back?' Jermaine asked sweetly, and, receiving a withering look for her trouble, was glad that Lukas and Ash were by then too close for any other private conversation.

The four of them ambled into the house, but Jermaine guessed she would be hearing more from her sister before too long. Only then did she realise that she should have given thought to how Edwina would react to her arriving so unexpectedly. It went without saying, of course, that she wouldn't like it. But, Jermaine realised, she had been so taken up with her happiness at just being with Lukas that she just hadn't given a solitary thought to how her sister

would react that Lukas had gone out on his own and had
returned with a passenger—complete with suitcase.

'Tea?' Lukas suggested.

Suddenly, ridiculously, probably because the other two
were there, Jermaine was swamped by an unexpected shyness. It was absurd, she freely admitted. But then, since
Cupid had released that powerfully potent arrow, she had
suffered various confidence-wrecking emotions which until
then she had been a total stranger to.

'I think I'll take my case up and...'

'I'll take it for you,' Ash insisted.

Jermaine looked across to Lukas; he smiled, and her
heart seemed to tilt. She managed to smile back, and then
Edwina was intruding on the moment with a friendly offer
of, 'I'll come and help you unpack, Jermaine.'

Feeling a touch startled, Jermaine switched her glance
from Lukas to her pleasantly smiling sister. Edwina didn't
intend to wait any longer to find out what the devil was
going on, apparently.

Ash led the way to the same bedroom Jermaine had used
before. It smelt clean and newly polished, and the bed,
which she had stripped on leaving the last time, was made
up with fresh linen. Jermaine smiled—Mrs Dobson obviously always liked to keep guest rooms aired and ready.

Ash did not stay long once he had deposited Jermaine's
case, but as he departed so too did any semblance of pleas-
antness from Edwina. 'What's with the sweet smiles?' she
demanded aggressively once the door was closed.

'Sweet smiles?' Jermaine echoed.

'You were damned near swooning at Lukas not two
minutes ago!'

Swooning? Oh, heavens, surely not? What must Lukas
think? 'Well, you'd know, with all the practice you've
had!' Jermaine refused to let her sister squash her spirit.

Edwina, plainly observing that Jermaine had no intention

of being pushed around, adopted another tack. 'How did you meet up with Lukas, anyway?' she demanded hostilely.

'He happened to call in…'

'On the parents!' That Edwina could hardly believe it was obvious.

'He was in the area and…'

'What for?'

'I don't know what for! I didn't ask!'

'You wouldn't!' Edwina scorned in disgust. But, not done yet, she carried on, 'You needn't have come back with him. I'll bet you asked. You fancy him, don't you. Well, hard luck, Jermaine. He wasn't giving you a thought last night when we…'

'You've brought this on yourself!' Jermaine cut in sharply. She just didn't want to hear what Edwina was saying. As ever, she would spoil everything for her if she could. 'And I didn't ask to come here with Lukas—Dad near enough did that.' Unfastening her case, Jermaine saw the gift she had brought her sister reposing there. She handed it to her. Edwina received the gift-wrapped bottle of her favourite perfume without thanks.

'Dad!' she exclaimed shortly. 'How? He…'

'He's still worried about your back. Even though only the evening before I'd mentioned Mrs Dobson being here, Dad seems to think you might be feeling uncomfortable without another woman around.' Unsmiling, Jermaine looked at her sister. 'Which just shows how little he really knows you,' she added acidly.

She saw Edwina's eyes narrow, and guessed she would be paid back for that sooner or later, but as Edwina went angrily from the room Jermaine sank winded on to the bed. Edwina, with her 'he wasn't giving you a thought last night when we…' had already put the poison down.

What *had* Lukas and Edwina done last night? Stop it, Jermaine demanded of herself. You know Edwina. She always has been able to embroider the truth—even lie out-right without so much as blinking. If whatever it was had been so wonderful, why had Lukas left Edwina on her own, or rather with Ash, today, while he conducted business out of the area?

Jermaine unpacked her case, trying to recapture the happiness of her time with Lukas in the snow—he hadn't been desperate to get back here to Edwina, Jermaine reminded herself. But that happiness eluded her. When, prior to her conversation with Edwina, Jermaine had felt she might well go back down the stairs again once she'd got her belongings stowed, now, somehow, she had no heart to go down to the drawing room. Yet she felt a need to be doing something other than pacing her room. Restlessly Jermaine considered popping along to the kitchen to see Mrs Dobson, but decided against it. The housekeeper would be up to her ears in things domestic at this hour.

Had not darkness descended, Jermaine would have given in to the urge to go and visit that tranquil spot by the brook—perhaps some of that peace and tranquillity would rub off on to her.

But winter's darkness *had* descended, and, as if to wash away the feelings of disquiet Edwina had sown with her intimate reference to her and Lukas last night, Jermaine went and stood under the shower, prior to getting ready to go down to dinner.

When, an hour later, good manners, if nothing else, decreed she could not stay skulking in her room until tomorrow, she was very much wishing she had never let Lukas persuade her to come.

But as she left her room she recalled the manner of Lukas persuading her to come, and his gently teasing 'What did I do? What did I say that makes you want to deprive me of your company' and her mood began to lighten. 'My dear, Jermaine' he'd called her. Oh, Lukas.

She saw him! He was standing at the bottom of the stairs as if waiting for her. Jermaine fought hard not to break out into smiles just to see him; Edwina's poison was still at work. But Jermaine's instinct belatedly roused itself to scoff that she should never have taken any heed of Edwina's half-sentences—good heavens, she'd grown up listening to Edwina making up anything to suit her own ends.

'You didn't come down,' Lukas accused as Jermaine reached him.

Her heart fluttered, thoughts of Edwina with Lukas a million miles away—Lukas sounded as if he'd waited and waited.

'I—er—I'm here now,' Jermaine managed.

'So you are,' he smiled, and took her into his arms and kissed her. Reluctantly, it seemed, he let her go. 'Don't you just love Christmas and all the mistletoe?' he asked softly. Jermaine looked up and just had to laugh out loud, because while she could not deny it was Christmas, and the hall was decorated with plenty of holly, she could not see so much as the merest sprig of mistletoe.

She still had laughter about her mouth when, somehow holding her hand, Lukas strolled with her to the drawing room. Nor did he seem in any hurry to let go of her hand when they went in. Edwina was already downstairs, decorating one of the sofas, Jermaine saw.

She also saw Edwina's eyes immediately laser to their entwined hands, and didn't miss the tightening of Edwina's mouth the moment before she broke out into girlish smiles and teased, 'Making an entrance again, Jermaine?'

Oh, how could she? Jermaine wondered if she was the only one to notice the barb beneath the smiles. 'What would you like to drink, Edwina?' Lukas asked, letting go Jermaine's hand. *Milk might suit.* 'Jermaine?' Having asked the elder Hargreaves sister, he turned to the younger one.

So the evening got underway, with Ash moving to sit next to Edwina, where he chatted pleasantly to her until it was time to go into the dining room.

Thankfully, the meal progressed without Edwina making any more barbed remarks under a smiling cover. Though Jermaine didn't miss the hard look Edwina couldn't immediately hide when she was not the object of Lukas's attention but Jermaine was.

Again Jermaine's emotions went all out of gear. For it seemed to her that when she was alone with Lukas she was able to forget all else. That she was able to trust him and to just enjoy being with him. She didn't even need to wonder where their friendship was going, be it nowhere at all— it was enough to be with him. But with Edwina there— though not so much Ash, funnily enough—Jermaine felt stilted, awkward, as if she had to watch every word... As if any minute now Edwina would pounce and spoil everything. Was she imagining it because she wanted it to be so, Jermaine wondered, or was it true that, while being the perfect host, Lukas looked *her* way more and more frequently? Almost—as if he was hard put to it to take his eyes off her.

Imagination, scoffed her love-filled heart. Though she had noticed that Edwina was watching all points and, to anyone who knew her as well as Jermaine, seemed to have her nose put out of joint.

That evening they had coffee at the dinner table, but returned to the drawing room afterwards. 'Would you like a drink of something to finish off with?' Lukas asked Edwina, who went through a pantomime of being unsure what she would like and so went over to the drinks cabinet with Lukas in order to choose.

Ash was all at once taking the seat next to Jermaine. 'I don't seem to have had a moment to talk to you alone.'

'Have you enjoyed your Christmas?' she asked, smiling

while her emotions see-sawed, because Edwina seemed captivated by something Lukas had just said to her.

'Can we be friends, Jermaine?' Ash, instead of answering her question, was asking one of his own.

Jermaine determinedly gave him her full attention. Ash seemed extremely serious suddenly. 'You sound as though it's important to you,' she commented lightly.

Ash stared solemnly at her. 'Actually, it is,' he answered. 'Though I wouldn't blame you if, after the way I treated you, you told me to get lost.'

Jermaine looked back into his sombre expression. 'Water under the bridge,' she smiled, and because he was Lukas's brother, and because she bore Ash no ill will, and would indeed like to be friends with him, she agreed sincerely, 'Friends.' She was about to extend her hand in friendship when Ash beamed a smile and kissed her—in friendship.

'Have lunch with me one day next week?' he suggested—but never received an answer, because suddenly Lukas was there, standing over them.

'What are you having to drink, Jermaine?' he cut in abruptly, in contrast to the pleasant way he'd been with her, all at once sounding quite aggressive.

If he asked like that, she'd die of thirst, rather. 'Nothing, thanks,' she answered politely, and could only think that Edwina had been putting more poison down—this time to Lukas. 'If no one minds,' she began, getting to her feet, 'I think I'll go to bed.'

'You're sure?' Ash was on his feet too. Lukas walked away.

'I'm sure,' she smiled, wished everyone a general 'Good-night,' and found she had her sister for company.

'I'm without my hanky, I'll just come up and get one,' Edwina trilled, and went with Jermaine out into the hall. 'Enjoying yourself?' she asked as they started up the staircase, for once fairly bubbling with good humour.

Jermaine's suspicions were aroused. All evening she'd been getting nothing but surreptitious ill-humoured looks from her sister. Yet suddenly, with no one there to witness, she was giving her the benefit of her sunnier side?

'What happened to cheer you up?' Jermaine asked with sisterly candour.

'Isn't he wonderful?' Edwina sighed, and Jermaine knew at once that she shouldn't have asked.

'Presumably we're not talking about Ash, here?'

'Lukas has just asked me to stay at Highfield for as long as I like,' Edwina answered, barely able to contain herself, and, smiling a sly smile at Jermaine, she added, 'Wouldn't you call that progress?'

Thankfully, at that moment they reached the top of the stairs. Jermaine felt too choked to answer and left Edwina to go to collect the hanky she had come up for while she went three doors down to her own room.

Jermaine owned that she felt near to tears, but she wouldn't cry! Oh, how she wished she had never come. Sledging in the snow, laughing, kissing with Lukas that day—suddenly it all seemed light years away. His manner to her just now—cold and aggressive—had been a huge contrast.

She started to get angry—she wasn't having this! First he used his charm on her, and then switched to Edwina! Jermaine started to grow more and more incensed. Who did he think he was, playing ducks and drakes with her emotions? Not that he knew so much about her emotions, of course. Nor did she want him to. But he must have gleaned that she liked him a little at least—or why would she have accepted to come here today?

Jermaine found then that she could not sustain her anger against Lukas, and it departed as swiftly as it had arrived. But she felt restless again, and was taking her fourth shower of the day when she paused to wonder—had Edwina been speaking the truth? Or was this just some more of her poison?

It was a fact that her sister had seemed riveted by every word Lukas had been uttering to her over by the drinks cabinet. But then Edwina could bat her eyes for England if she wanted something. Could it be that, perhaps from some small word Lukas had said, Edwina had picked up her crewel needle and begun yet more fabricated embroidery?

Jermaine recalled the way Lukas had taken her in his arms and kissed her when she'd earlier left her room. She remembered also the moments during dinner, when he would look over to her, and had appeared to enjoy having her there.

She was nightdress-clad and in bed when she wondered if she could trust her instincts. Could she trust that feeling that—well, that Lukas sort of liked her—well, a lot—in the romantic way?

But that was when she also remembered how she had trusted his brother, Ash, and Jermaine came down to earth with a very hard landing. Oh, great! Realising that she must be the biggest chump going, and that the philandering Tavinor brothers were having a fine old time at her expense, Jermaine was all set to leap out of bed, get dressed and get out of there right that minute.

Someone tapping lightly on her door took the moment from her. She picked up her watch—it was comparatively early; not quite ten-thirty yet. She didn't think this Boxing Day night that anyone else was retiring yet, and in the next second she was out of bed. Rapidly tying in her robe as she went, she streaked over to answer the door. It wouldn't be Edwina. She wouldn't knock, but would come straight in. But if this was one of the Tavinor twosome, she was ready for him—the one who wanted to be her friend or the other one, who'd said he'd 'missed' her and called her 'my dear.'

Angrily she pulled back the door—and her ridiculous heart wobbled. 'Yes?' she demanded coldly—and for her sins had to stand there and endure his scrutiny.

'I knew I'd upset you,' Lukas said quietly.

'Pfuff!' she exhaled on a careless breath.

Lukas smiled deep into her stormy violet eyes. 'According to my old nanny, one should never go to sleep on an argument.'

'We didn't argue!' Jermaine reminded him pithily. She didn't want him to smile; it weakened her.

'Are you going to let me apologise?' he asked nicely, and she was weakened further. She wanted time alone with him, she so desperately wanted to be back the way they had been.

'Forget it,' she said stubbornly, and started to close the door.

'You kissed my brother!' Lukas reminded her urgently.

'When?' she answered, startled, the door still open.

'Not long since—in the drawing room.'

She stared at him. He'd been aggressive, cold to her—because of that kiss? Her heartbeat picked up speed. Somehow she managed to get herself back together. 'I didn't kiss him. He kissed me.'

'You're not going to have lunch with him, are you?' Lukas asked winningly, and a staggering thought suddenly stunned her.

'You're—not...' she hardly dared voice the word '...jealous?'

'Me?' Lukas scoffed. But when she was ready to run at the mortification she felt from what she'd just voiced, Lukas answered, self-deprecatingly, 'Just because my brother was sitting chatting to you, just because he was kissing you?'

He *was* jealous! Her heart started to thunder, and any anger she had felt melted into nothing. Oh, he couldn't be jealous—could he? She tried hard to keep both feet firmly on the ground. 'He—Ash—wants us to be friends,' Jermaine replied, having been through the agonies of jealousy herself, not wanting that pain for the man she loved.

'Ah!' said Lukas—just as though that explained everything.

But Jermaine was starting to backtrack on her notion that Lukas might be at all jealous in any way—and began to feel awkward that she had actually suggested to his face that he might be.

'Goodnight, then,' she bade him, and would have closed the door, but again his words stopped her.

'Don't you want to see your Christmas present?' he asked, and while Jermaine stared witlessly at him Lukas bent to the side of the door that had been hidden from her view and picked up a square, flattish parcel. 'Happy Christmas, Jermaine,' he wished her softly, handing her the gold-wrapped parcel.

'Oh, Lukas!' she wailed. 'I didn't get you anything!'

'Don't be upset. My gift is supposed to make you happy,' he teased.

'May I open it?'

He nodded, a warm light in his grey eyes as he studied her face, but as a welter of emotions began to fluster her Jermaine had to turn from him. She didn't want him looking into her eyes, seeing her very soul. She walked back into her room, her fingers busy with the gold wrapping.

She removed the first wrapping to find that, whatever her gift was, it was protected by a firmer second wrapper. But once that had been done away with a gasp of utter astonishment broke from her. 'Lukas!' she cried, and spun round to stare at him open-mouthed. 'You...' she gasped, but was rendered speechless by the unexpectedness of his gift.

He had closed the door and had stepped a little way inside her room. 'You like it?' He smiled, her incredulous expression already telling him that 'like it' was an under-statement.

Jermaine's violet gaze went from him and back to the painting he had given her. 'It's the *Boy With A Barrow!*' she told him what he already knew. 'We saw it at that art gallery...' Her voice tailed off. 'I can't take it!' she exclaimed suddenly.

'You *don't* like it?'

'Oh, Lukas, you know that I love it. It's the most marvellous Christmas present ever,' she replied honestly, huskily. 'But it must have been expensive, and I can't...'

'Oh, my lovely girl, you can,' Lukas interrupted gently. 'May I not have the pleasure of seeing you enjoy your picture?' Her picture! Jermaine's eyes grew dreamy. That sounded so personal, somehow. As if—as if whenever Lukas had looked at the picture he had thought of it as her picture. 'I promise you it wasn't so very expensive,' Lukas went on to assure her when she still looked uncertain. And, for a killer punch, 'You must know, sweet Jermaine, that I couldn't possibly allow anyone else to have it.'

Her backbone went to water. 'Oh, Lukas!' she cried tremulously.

'You're not going to cry?' he asked, looking a shade worried and coming further into her room.

She laughed. 'I'm going to kiss you,' she said.

'Of the two, I can bear that better,' he grinned—and held his arms out to her.

Jermaine took one last look at the blue and pink, and the touch of red in the painting, then carefully put it down. With the whole of her being starting to tremble, she went into Lukas's outstretched arms.

His mouth against her own was the salve she needed for her earlier unhappiness. In the harbour of his arms all feeling of restlessness vanished. One kiss became two, and as

Lukas held her firmly to him so she wanted more and more of him. He did not seem in any hurry to let her go.

Soon passion began to flare between them, going from warm, to hot, to fire, as Lukas traced kisses down the side of her throat and pressed her to him. She arched to him, and a murmur of wanting left him. She felt him, his body heat through the thinness of her robe, felt his hands low on her waist, at the curves of her behind as he pulled her into him.

'Lukas!' she gasped, delight such as she'd never experienced shooting through her body.

Lukas pulled back to look into the depths of her lovely violet eyes, his grey ones smouldering with his desire for her. 'We should stop?' he asked her throatily.

She swallowed hard. She didn't want to stop. She wanted more of his kisses, more of his touch. 'Do—we have to?' she asked.

'My darling!' he breathed, and as Jermaine's heart leapt, so she knew that she was ready, eager, to go wherever he led.

She smiled up at him, and as she leaned forward and kissed him so Lukas lifted her up and carried her to the bed, and gently laid her down upon it. She knew that he would join her. It was what she wanted.

She closed her eyes, her heart full. She felt the bed go down, and as Lukas came to lie beside her she opened them again and saw he had shrugged out of his jacket. He took her in his arms and they clung to each other. It was bliss, pure and simple, to be this close, to feel his body heat.

Again and again they kissed, and, as his hands caressed her so her hands seemed to roam of their own volition over his back and shoulders. Gently his seeking hands moved to her breasts, and she realised he must have heard her shaky breath.

'You're not frightened, sweetheart?' he asked.

'No,' she whispered. 'No,' she repeated, fearful he might not have heard the first time and might stop making love to her. 'Just a bit—um—shy, I think.'

Gently, tenderly, he laid his lips on hers. 'Sweet, Jermaine,' he breathed against her mouth, parting her lips with his own. Slowly, as if not to hurry her in this momentous happening for her, Lukas's hands went to the tie of her robe. 'May I?' He was still giving her all the time in the world to back away if she was in the least unsure.

'Yes,' she answered, and loved him, loved him, loved him, as gently he removed her robe.

Her nightdress had ridden up and Jermaine felt her face flame when she felt Lukas's hands underneath her nightdress, felt his warm touch on her bare upper thigh.

'L-Lukas!' she whispered tremulously.

His hand stilled, but there was nothing but tender understanding in his sensitive grey eyes. 'You're not quite so sure?' he asked, looking down into her lovely violet eyes, her love-flushed face.

'I am,' she assured him as quickly as she could, given that her throat felt dry. 'It's—it's just—it's all a bit—um—new, that's...'

'I know, sweetheart,' he said. 'It will be all right. Trust me.'

'Oh, I do,' she sighed, and kissed him lovingly, and had not the slightest demur to make when his stilled hand moved upwards under her nightdress, and, taking her breath with the delight of his touch, his warm, searching hand roamed her belly and upwards, to capture the swollen globe of her breast. 'Oh!' she sighed.

'You're not afraid?'

She wanted to tell him that because she loved him so everything seemed so right. 'Not with you,' she said shyly.

'My darling!' Lukas breathed exultantly, and for long, delicious moments he kissed and caressed her. Apart from a natural shyness, Jermaine was in utter rapture when he carefully took from her her last covering. 'You are a delight, sweet love,' he murmured as he gazed into her eyes, a moment before he feasted his eyes on her pink-tipped breasts. 'Oh, my Jermaine,' he murmured throatily, and Jermaine knew yet more bliss when he trailed kisses down to her breast. While one hand held, caressed and moulded her right breast, he caressed her left breast with his mouth.

Jermaine knew further enchantment when, with one arm holding her close, his sensitive fingers at her breast teased the hardened peak, cupping her breast, while his tongue at her other breast made a nonsense of her as he tasted its sweet fullness.

Again they kissed, and held and kissed, and caressed and kissed—and suddenly, in her enchanted world, Jermaine all at once became aware that Lukas had removed his clothes and was lying completely naked next to her.

'Lukas!' she cried shakily, instinctively pulling back.

'You're shocked?' he asked.

'No, no. I...' She didn't know where she was, what to do, what to say. 'Help me,' she begged.

He pulled a little away from her. 'You want to make love with me, little darling?'

'Y-yes,' she answered on a thread of sound.

'But?' He seemed to sense there was a hint of hesitation there.

'But nothing,' she answered, and swallowed hard a moment before she begged, 'Kiss me, please kiss me.'

'Sweet love,' Lukas murmured, and bent to kiss her, their bodies close once more. Jermaine clutched hard on to him, the physical feel of him, his skin, next to her on-fire skin, causing her to need a second to adjust. Biology lessons had never prepared her for this moment of being so acutely aware of a man and his need.

'Lukas,' she breathed his name jerkily. But just then the crash of a door slamming somewhere, so out of place in this moment of deep and sensitive loving, caused her to jump in alarm. And all at once Lukas was making a decision which she didn't want him to make. He sat up fast, pulling away from her. While she hadn't a clue what was happening, he began to speedily don his undergarment and trousers—so speedily it was as if, if he didn't hurry, he might change his mind. 'What?' Jermaine questioned, sitting up too.

'This isn't right, for you, my love,' Lukas said, turning to look at her, his glance flicking down to her breasts and hastily away again.

'It isn't?'

She saw a muscle jerk in his jaw. 'I thought it was. I thought we...' He broke off, and then, obviously referring to the banging of the door that had made her jump, 'But there's too much traffic... We need to be totally alone somewhere, where I can...' He broke off again, his glance seeking hers. 'Do you 1...care for me?' he asked, and suddenly his eyes were steady on hers.

Jermaine wanted to tell him that he was the whole world to her, but, sitting there as naked as the day she was born, she was suddenly overwhelmed by shyness.

She realised that Lukas had seen her shyness when, 'Come here,' he breathed, and took her gently into his arms and held her, her breasts pressed against his hair roughened naked chest. Then, gently, he put her from him. 'That wasn't such a great idea,' he admitted with a crooked kind of grin. And holding her firmly by her upper arms, he admitted, 'Being with you here, like this, is just too much, sweetheart. I'm having trouble thinking straight.' Determinedly he moved away from her, and, when all Jermaine wanted to do was to lie with him through the night, he said, 'If you care anything for me, my love, meet me tomorrow—away from this room…' He paused, then smiled. 'I'll wait for you on our bench. Do you know where I mean?'

'By the bridge, the brook?' she answered huskily.

'Nine sharp,' he said, then changed his mind. 'No, I can't wait that long. Eight-thirty?'

Jermaine desperately wanted to say 'eight,' but her heart was pounding wildly and—was Lukas saying *he cared* about her?—she wasn't thinking very straight herself. 'Half past eight,' she agreed.

'Oh, my darling,' he groaned, every bit as if he had gleaned from her agreement to meet him that care she did. 'I'm going,' he said firmly. 'While I still can.' He looked at her, and Jermaine folded her arms defensively in front of her bare breasts. 'You're absolutely exquisite,' he said softly, quickly kissed her—and was gone.

CHAPTER NINE

JERMAINE barely slept that night. Yet even awake she felt as if she was dreaming. 'Our bench' Lukas had said. Their bench. If she was dreaming, what a wonderful, wonderful dream it was.

Again and again she recalled his tenderness, the gentle endearments he had murmured while making love to her. Was she his sweet love, his darling, his sweetheart? Oh, she so wanted to be.

She tried hard for logic, tried hard not to believe what she wanted to believe. Admittedly, she didn't know very much about it, but weren't men apt to say anything in the heat of lovemaking?

But—she changed her mind—she didn't want to listen to logic. Besides, even desiring her as he undoubtedly had—and here her insides were all of a mish-mash as she recalled their mutual desire as they'd lain naked together—Lukas was more sincere than that. Somehow she instinctively seemed to know that, even while he desired her, he would never, even should his physical need try to rule him, say something he did not mean.

Which—her heart gave a flutter—must mean, if she trusted her instinct, that when Lukas said, 'If you care anything for me,' he in turn must care a little something for her. Oh, could she believe that? She so wanted to. Why else, if he didn't care for her, would Lukas want to meet her away from the house?

There was too much traffic in the house, he'd said. Which must mean that he wanted to be alone with her— away from the house. Didn't that then mean that he wanted to talk to her? No way did he want them to meet away from the house so that they could make love. Jermaine smiled at the thought. Lukas was hardly likely to get amorous sitting on that bench with snow all around. So—what did he want to talk to her about?

Her brain refused to go any further, to speculate, to hope. She began to feel all of a tremble inside, and couldn't stay in bed any longer. By seven o'clock she had been up ages. She was showered, dressed, had light make-up applied, in fact she was all ready to go—and had an hour and a half to wait.

But by the time half past seven came around she was in a hopeless muddle of differing emotions. She couldn't sit; she couldn't stand still. She took to constantly looking at the painting Lukas had given her, but was in such a turmoil she could not concentrate on seeing more in the painting than she already had.

She loved her gift. It was so personal. She had no idea when he had bought it, but it had to have been before last night. Lukas had bought it especially for her—had meant it for her because he knew that she had been so taken with it. Did that mean that he cared a little for her? Or was she being totally stupid?

At eight o'clock she felt she could not take walking up and down her room, combing her hair, checking she looked all right, washing her hands and lingering over her painting for much longer.

It was ten past eight when, by then in too much of an agitated state to stay in her room another minute—yet not wanting to appear too eager if she had got everything impossibly wrong by going to that bench twenty minutes ahead of time—Jermaine had the vague idea of perhaps popping into the kitchen and whiling away some time with Mrs Dobson.

To Jermaine then it seemed about the only decision she

was capable of making, and, remembering the way that door had slammed last night, she was desperate not to disturb the whole household. It would just about finish her if she had got everything totally muddled and wrong, and she alerted Lukas to the fact she couldn't wait to see him and was leaving her room so much ahead of time.

Silently, hardly breathing, Jermaine left her room, closing the door without a sound. She was fully aware that her sister never surfaced before nine, so was taken by surprise when, almost at Edwina's room, Jermaine spotted that the door stood wide open!

In two minds about retreating back to her own room—she had other things in her head besides doing battle with Edwina if she was on the prowl about something and was watching for her to pass—Jermaine almost did an about-turn. But she had already spent enough time pacing up and down, and perhaps Edwina wouldn't spot her.

Edwina did spot her though—she looked directly at her through half-closed eyes. But as a smirk of a smile tweaked Edwina's mouth, and she closed her eyes and her expression became dreamy, it was all too clear that she had other concerns than baiting her younger sister. But that did not stop Jermaine from feeling pole-axed. Because Edwina was not alone!

Feeling totally shattered, the colour draining from her face, Jermaine just couldn't believe what her eyes were telling her. For there, holding her sister aloft in his arms, was the man with whom Jermaine had an assignation in twenty minutes' time!

Staggered beyond bearing, Jermaine was incapable of moving, and so had to stand and watch while the man who less than twelve hours ago had picked her up and carried her over to her bed, now carried her dreamy-expressioned sister over to *her* bed!

Stunned, reeling, it was only the thought that she too

must have worn pretty much the self-same expression that Edwina was wearing now that maliciously stabbed Jermaine into life.

Ten minutes after that and she was coming out of shock to realise she was back in her room and that, quite without being fully aware of what she had been doing, she had tossed her belongings into her case and was ready to leave.

Her eyes lit on her painting, the one she had so idiotically allowed herself to believe Lukas had purchased for her because he had some liking for her. The pain that hit her then was almost physical. She looked away from the painting, looked out through the window, absently seeing that Ash had just brought his car round to the front of the house from the garages at the rear.

He had got out and was using some de-icing device when Jermaine suddenly came out of her only half-aware state and was all at once galvanised into action.

When Jermaine left her room, she left behind her picture. She didn't want to think. To think hurt too much. But she knew without thinking that she could not take with her the picture that had meant so much to her and so little to him.

The door to Edwina's room was now closed. Jermaine sprinted past it, only just holding down a sob. Was he still in there with her? Were they laughing together at the thought that the stupid virgin would shortly be out there, sitting waiting on a bench in the snow, while the man Jermaine would be waiting for was very patently *busy* elsewhere?

Unable to bear the nightmare flashes in her head, of Lukas lying with Edwina in the same way he had lain with her last night, Jermaine hung onto a thread of sanity and raced out of there. It was that or go storming into that room to have a few short, sharp words with the venomous snake Lukas Tavinor.

Ash was in the driving seat about to pull away when

Jermaine hared out through the front door. She was suddenly too incensed to be aware if the case she hauled with her weighed two pounds or two hundred.

'Jermaine!' Ash exclaimed, getting out of the vehicle when he saw her white and anguished face. 'What...?'

'Would you take me to the nearest railway station?' she cut in without more ado.

'But, sweetheart...'

My stars, they were both at it! 'I'll walk!' she snapped.

Ash moved. He moved fast and grabbed her case from her. 'Get in,' he said, and, going round to the passenger door, he opened it for her. 'What...?' he began again.

'If you really want to be my friend—as you last night wanted to be—you'll drive on without questioning me!' she told him tautly—and didn't breathe freely again until after Ash had started up the vehicle and had driven half a mile away from Highfield.

She was aware then that Ash had been glancing at her from time to time, but it was about five minutes later when he glanced at her again and assured her, 'Believe me, Jermaine, I'm not trying to pry. I can tell you're upset. But may I know why you need to get to a railway station?'

She would have thought that was obvious. 'I'm going home,' she replied bluntly.

'To your parents?'

Oh, grief. If she went back there, her father would go on and on about her leaving Edwina on her own. The way she was feeling, Jermaine didn't think she would be able to refrain from telling him a few home truths about his elder pride and joy.

'To my home, my flat,' she answered, and found that Ash had been speaking the truth about being her friend when he insisted that he would drive her back to London.

'The trains may not have resumed a full service after the

holiday yet,' he reasoned. But added after a moment or two's thought, 'Though I'll need to fill up with petrol first.'

Jermaine realised she was putting him to a great deal of trouble, but with Lukas and his treachery spinning around and around in her head she could only feel grateful to Ash for getting her away from Highfield and that cold-hearted monster.

It had gone nine when Ash finally found a petrol station that was open. 'I won't be long,' he said, opening the door after filling up and pointing to the office, where he was going to pay.

She followed his direction, but as weak tears suddenly, unexpectedly, pricked the back of her eyes, she looked away. Pride rushed to the fore, decreeing that no one should see exactly what Lukas Tavinor had done to her.

'Take as long as you like,' she said as brightly as she could, which wasn't all that bright in reality, and as Ash went to settle the account she stared out of the car window, unseeing of anything as the pain of Lukas and his duplicity started to get through the barrier she was trying to erect.

Ash could have been away two minutes, or twenty. Her head was so full of Lukas, of the way they had been with each other last night. For all she knew, he could have last night gone straight from her room to Edwina's.

Ash had started up the car when a shaken dry sob caught Jermaine out. She quickly turned it into a cough, but saw Ash glance swiftly at her. 'Jermaine, I...' he began, as if her cough hadn't fooled him at all.

'Don't, Ash,' she said tightly.

'All right, love,' he agreed, but went on, 'Er—do you mind if we don't go on the motorway?' Adding, before she could answer, 'The thing is, while naturally I'm only too pleased to take you anywhere you want to go, I was on my way to do an errand across country.'

Jermaine managed to find a smile. 'I'm truly grateful to

you, Ash,' she replied, when what she really wanted to do was to get back to her flat with all speed, close the door, and perhaps keep it that way until it was time for her to return to work. 'Please do your errand first. I'm in no hurry,' she assured him.

The errand Ash had to do added about forty minutes to the journey. He pulled up outside a house out in the wilds somewhere. 'I won't be long,' he promised, and, true to his word, was soon back.

They were further delayed, though, because Ash didn't want to risk going too fast with the roads still snow laden in parts. To Jermaine's mind, Ash was being excessively cautious. But, she owned, he probably wasn't. It just seemed that way because of her urgent need to be somewhere by herself, where she could lick her wounds in private.

Her head was still besieged with everything that had taken place in the last twenty-four hours when they reached London. Why, oh, why had Lukas called at her parents' home yesterday? Why, when he was so obviously enamoured of Edwina, had he not ignored her father's broadest of hints that he take his younger daughter back to Highfield with him?

Memories of the wonderful time they had shared sledging in the snow tried to get a foothold. She pushed them angrily away. That time was as phoney as Tavinor was phoney.

All she'd been to him was a challenge, a challenge to his male ego; she saw that now. My stars, how could she have been so blind? Had she so soon forgotten his reaction, his 'get thee behind me, Satan' when she'd more or less told him she hadn't yet met the man who would make her want to make love with him?

He hadn't been able to resist the temptation to put her to the test, had he? He'd even put aside his preference for

Edwina for a short while. Jermaine swallowed down another dry sob as she recalled how she had been his for the taking last night. He had known that too—test over.

Would he have made complete love to her, had not that door slamming brought him to an awareness that he had another, more experienced and therefore more exciting, willing woman three doors down...?

Jermaine abruptly snatched her mind back from where it was going. She didn't think she could take much more without breaking down, and if that happened she wanted to be somewhere on her own.

Thankfully, a minute later and Ash was pulling up outside where she lived. 'Thanks, Ash,' she said, when on the pavement he extracted her case. 'I'll ring you about that lunch,' she added, out of a need to part from him cheerfully.

'I'll carry your case in for you,' he answered.

'There's no need.' She was talking to his back, and there was nothing she could do but follow him and extract her keys from her bag.

She unlocked the outer door. But when she stretched out her hand for her case, Ash opened the door and went in first. Oddly, instead of making for the stairs once he was inside, he glanced about and, though he knew the way to her flat from the days when they'd used to see each other, he did no more than place her case down on the hall floor.

But, since nothing would surprise her any more—or so she'd thought—Jermaine didn't take much heed, until she suddenly heard him say, 'Been here long?' She turned to see whom he was addressing—and what little colour she had drained completely from her face.

'Thanks, Ash,' Lukas answered. *Lukas!*

Totally and utterly stunned, Jermaine stared at Lukas, vaguely realising that one of the other occupants of the building—most likely having recognised him from a previous visit—must have let him in. But that wasn't important. Because as she stared at Lukas she started to sense that something was going on between him and his brother—Ash didn't seem at all surprised to see Lukas there.

She switched her gaze from Lukas to Ash, 'You *phoned* him?' she accused, bringing out the only logical thought in any of this—while more logic questioned why on earth Ash would do anything of the sort. 'You rang him on your mobile from that garage!' she exclaimed, even as she wondered why, anyway, would Lukas, in response to that call, beat all records to get here before them?

'Make yourself scarce, Ash,' Lukas suggested evenly to him before he could answer her.

'You'll be all right, Jermaine,' Ash looked at her to promise.

'I won't hurt her,' Lukas assured him—and Jermaine came hurtling out of her trance, suddenly outraged.

'That's right, you won't!' she yelled. 'You're both leaving!'

Ash looked doubtful. Lukas settled the matter by ignoring the fact that Jermaine had a murderous kind of glint in her eyes and escorting his brother to the door.

'Be in touch—soon,' Ash requested.

'I will,' Lukas assured him quietly, let his brother out from the building and then, turning slowly around, he looked Jermaine steadily in the eye. 'Now,' he challenged harshly, refusing to let her look away, 'what have you got to say for yourself?'

CHAPTER TEN

WHAT had she got to say for herself? Of all the confounded nerve! Fuming, her eyes flashing fire, Jermaine glared at him. She had expected, before this, that she would feel nothing for Lukas—that her feelings for him would die an instant death the moment she learned of his double-dealing with her sister. It had always happened before. But this time it had not. When she would by far prefer not to, Jermaine found that she still loved the perfidious rat.

'What do you mean what have I got to say for myself?' she flew, enraged. Love him she might, but at this very moment she felt very much like burying something large and sharp in his head.

His steady gaze did not waver, but when, just then, one of her neighbours began to emerge from further down the hall, Lukas enquired, his tone tough and uncompromising, 'Do your want to go the full twelve rounds out here?'

She didn't. She was hurting, and she felt humiliated enough without having half the apartment block knowing all about it. 'Close the door on your way out!' she tossed at him hostilely, and made for the stairs.

She had forgotten her case, but she was too proud to go back down for it while he was still in the building. Evidence that he was still in the building—and she was looking nowhere but straight in front—was there in the fact that, to show her what he thought of her hostile dismissal, Lukas kept pace with her as she stormed up every stair. He was carrying her large case too.

It came in handy for him when, reaching her door, she unlocked it intending to go in, do a swift about-turn and shut the door on him. It didn't work out that way, because as she went to shut the door—she discovered that her suitcase was wedged in the doorway.

Jermaine threw Lukas a speaking look and turned her back on him. It did not surprise her that he followed her, uninvited, into her home. She heard the door close as she walked into her sitting room. She was not feeling any more friendly to him when, reaching the middle of her carpet, she spun round to face him.

'Well?' she snapped. The nerve of him! The utter, villainous nerve of him!

Her fury, it seemed, was not lost on him. He even seemed a bit put out himself, she realised, as he grated, 'I don't know what the hell you're so wild about!' The audacity of it! 'I was the one who was stood up!'

'Stood up?' she echoed—she didn't believe this! He thought he could fool around with her *and* her sister and...

'We had a date, you and me,' he snarled forthrightly—should she require any reminding.

Ooh, was he asking for it—right between the eyes. 'As I remember it, there was a proviso on that arrangement!' she flared. 'It went something along the lines of "If you care anything for me".' Didn't she know the words off by heart? Hadn't she relived them, been enraptured by them all through that long night as she'd waited for dawn to come? But—suddenly she was aware that Lukas seemed badly shaken.

'You're saying you care nothing for me?' he asked tautly.

'There—I always knew you were intelligent,' she lobbed back sarcastically. She wanted him to go. Her anger was on the wane and she was starting to hurt again.

Lukas stared at her unspeaking for some tense moments, then he took a deep and controlling breath. And then, very clearly, he clipped, 'I don't believe you.'

Anger, born of panic that he might see just how deeply she did care for him, became her ally again. 'I don't give a button what you believe!' she hurled back at him fiercely.

'You'd have me think you were the way you were with me last night—and didn't care for me?' Trust him to bring that up! 'You'd have me believe you didn't care for me whatsoever, yet would have given me what you've given no man?'

'Charming!' she derided.

'You deny it?'

She wished she could. He knew her too well, it seemed. She turned away, presenting him with her back. 'Why have you come?' she asked dully—and started to feel more churned up inside than ever when she realised he must have taken a couple of steps closer to her. For his voice was directly behind her when he answered.

'I've come, basically, because I find it too difficult, too hard, to contemplate that you have no feelings for me at all. I've come because...'

'Don't,' she stopped him. 'Don't, Lukas.' She drew a shaky breath that was a half-sob, and supposed he must have heard it, for the next she knew he had taken an urgent hold of her shoulders. She shrugged him angrily away. 'I *saw* you!' she cried on a flare of anger, her emotions riding high.

'Saw me?' Lukas questioned, taking his hands from her at the distress he picked up in her voice. 'What do you mean, saw me?'

'I'm used to being the "also ran" when men see Edwina as the better option,' Jermaine answered, striving mightily to keep herself together. 'I just foolishly thought—thought—oh, never mind!' she snapped. For heavens' sake, she'd nearly told him that she'd thought he might prefer her, rather than her sister. Almost told him that she'd thought he was different from the others—indicating that he was special. Good heavens—Jermaine went hot all over—she'd nearly told him that she'd thought that there was something special between her and him—the two of them!

She took a step from him, but before she could go any further Lukas caught a hold of her, and this time when she went to shrug him off he refused to let her go. What was more, it appeared he had grown tired of not being able to read her face, her eyes. For, regardless of her resistance, he began to slowly turn her until at last she was facing him. When she stubbornly refused to look at him he, as obstinately, if gently, placed a hand beneath her chin and brought her head up.

His grey eyes searched into her wounded violet eyes for some seconds, then, very quietly, he said, 'But I do mind, Jermaine.'

'Tough!' she retaliated, but it was a weak effort. She wanted to oppose him, all the way she wanted to oppose him, only it didn't seem so easy now that he was here, in this very room, with her, his eyes holding hers. She supposed she might still be suffering from the shock of seeing him so unexpectedly.

'So you saw me,' Lukas took up, ignoring her opposition and seeming determined to get sorted that for which he must have sped all the way along the motorway to get sorted. 'And this has to have something to do with your sister, or you wouldn't have mentioned her...' He broke off, his brow suddenly shooting back as clearly something he hadn't thought of struck him. 'Oh, my love,' he mourned. 'You saw me in Edwina's bedroom this morning!'

'Too true, I did,' Jermaine answered coldly. How *dare* he call her his love?

'Why didn't you come in and...?'

'That depraved I'm not!' Jermaine erupted volcanically,

giving him a violent shove—to no avail. For it seemed, with his hands clamped to her upper arms, that he had not the smallest intention of letting her go. What was more, it looked as though he was starting to get angry himself. The sauce of it!

'What the hell do you think I am that…?' he began to rage—but she wasn't having that!

'Don't you come the holier than thou with me!' she cut in furiously. 'You'd already asked Edwina to stay at Highfield for as long as she liked, and the next thing I know,' she charged on, feeling more and more outraged by the second, 'is that you're in her room, carrying her to her bed, the same way you were in *my* room last night…' Hot colour surged to her cheeks. '…last night carrying me to *my* bed!' Lukas tried to get a word in, but Jermaine was in too much of an uproar by then to let him utter so much as a syllable. 'And we both know what happened then—what would have happened,' she tore into him, 'had not that door slammed somewhere and brought you to the realisation that there was a more experienced, more exciting female a few doors down who…'

'How dare you think that of me?' Lukas interrupted her on a bellow of sound—about the only way he could get a word in—and Jermaine had never seen him so explosively angry. His hands were biting into her arms as 'Hell's teeth!' he raged. 'I *knew* you were different, *knew* you were…' He broke off and, as if striving to put a rein on his fury, took a deep breath—and only then, while still holding her there in front of him, did he release some of the pressure on her arms. Then he took another long-drawn, controlling breath and, looking straight into her eyes, he more calmly stated, 'The only reason I tore myself away from you last night was because making love for the first time will be very special for you.' Her face flamed, and a hint of a smile touched his otherwise serious expression. 'I wanted you to know...' He stopped, then went on, 'I didn't want to rush you—knew I wanted to be alone with you, without interruption. Then that door crashed and gave me pause to realise that if you and your sister are like my brother and me, Edwina could waltz into your bedroom at any time—without bothering to knock. My home seemed crowded suddenly. I...'

At that juncture Jermaine came to an abrupt awareness that his talk of their lovemaking had made her all weak and spineless, causing her to be in danger of believing his every treacherous word. 'No wonder it was crowded—you'd invited too many people to stay!' she flew.

Lukas didn't care for being interrupted either; she saw that from the tightening of his fabulous mouth. But, when she was sure he would cast her to the devil and go rushing back to Edwina, he surprised her by staying exactly where he was and admitting, 'Yes, I did ask your sister to stay a few days longer at Highfield...' He broke off again when Jermaine struggled to be free, but held her firm and doggedly went on, 'But only for the same reason I extended the Christmas invitation to her in the first place. I...'

'I don't need to hear all the gory details.' Jermaine chopped him off disdainfully.

He didn't like that either, she saw, as his jaw jutted, but still he refused to let her go. 'You're going to hear anyway,' he told her bluntly. 'My oath, never have I met such a woman!' he muttered.

'You can say goodbye any time you like!'

'Shut up and listen.' She objected to being told to shut up, but before she could acquaint him, vitriolically, with her objections, he was going on, 'Believe me, and I don't mean to be unkind, but I'd had more than enough of your sister before...'

'It looked like it!'

Lukas tossed her a killing look, but, as determined to

have his say as Jermaine was determined not to shut up, it seemed, he pressed on, 'The only reason I tolerated her at all was because, having assured Ash that my home was his home while he searched for the right property to buy, I didn't want to alienate him by showing her the door. Their relationship looked serious in those first few days—for all I knew, he was planning on making her my sister-in-law. I think a lot of him,' he understated. 'I could put up with her if I had to.'

'Oh, the hardships you have to bear!'

He ignored her comment as if she hadn't spoken, but Jermaine didn't miss the glint in his eyes. Manfully, he controlled what he was feeling, albeit that he had to take a steadying breath. But he promptly proceeded to startle her when he went on, 'I've put up with that woman when I've known from almost the beginning that there was absolutely nothing wrong with her back. I've...'

'You knew she was faking?' Jermaine gasped, shock causing the words to rush from her. 'I mean...' Jermaine tried to recover, feeling guilty at having admitted her sister was a fraud.

Lukas's expression softened. 'You're so loyal to her, my love, but I knew you'd rumbled her from almost the start. That, of course, was the real reason why you refused to come and look after her.'

'I'd—er—phoned her on her mobile,' Jermaine found herself confessing.

'So you knew, before you even saw her, that she didn't require you in attendance?' Jermaine thought she had been disloyal enough, and did not answer. He continued, 'I think it was around then that my once clear and logical thinking started to get a little cloudy.'

'It—did?' Jermaine found herself questioning. She didn't want to ask questions. She wanted him to go—didn't she? But, equally, she wanted not to love him. Always before when she had known herself betrayed she had lost interest in a moment. So why wasn't it happening now?

'It did,' Lukas confirmed, and Jermaine felt all wobbly inside and in need of some severe stiffening of her backbone when, still holding her, Lukas moved her over to her sofa and sat down with her. She wanted to say something sarcastic—such as, Feeling tired?—but as Lukas had stayed here this long when she felt certain he had already endured enough of her acid, further barbs seemed to have temporarily deserted her. 'It was logical, to my mind,' he took up, when he could see that for once she wasn't going to interrupt, 'when Edwina refused to see a doctor or have a nurse—not that she needed either—that one of her relatives should come to Highfield to fetch and carry for her.'

'You weren't having Mrs Dobson doing it,' Jermaine put in.

Lukas smiled. 'We're on the same wavelength at last,' he said softly. But he was determined, it seemed, to tell it how it was.

'You ordered me to come and look after my sister.'

'And you let me know what you thought about that!' He paused. 'I own, sweet Jermaine, that I'm not used to women treating me like that.'

'You didn't care for it?' Why was she smiling back at him? This man was a treacherous toad!

'Why should I? Why, too, should I be irked every time I thought of you? How dared this woman talk to me like that—this woman with a beautiful voice who didn't care who the devil I was if she felt like going for my jugular. You actually told me to go and play with my train set,' he reminded her. 'Can you not see that after that, while of course I wasn't at all interested in you, I decided to come and see you? I left this apartment that night having met a most stunning-looking woman, but a woman whose attitude had annoyed me intensely. Was it any wonder I was unable to put you out of my mind?'

Her heart did a crazy kind of somersault—Lukas thought her stunning-looking! But Jermaine forced herself to remember his duplicity with her sister only that morning. Although somehow her trust in him was starting to kick in, and something, some instinct, was telling her to hear him out—she could trip him up later.

'Was that why you went to tell my parents about Edwina?'

He had the grace to look a smidgen abashed, but revealed, 'I was chatting to Ash when I got back to Highfield about some business I had near Oxford the next day. He told me Edwina's parents lived in that area.' Lukas hesitated, then added, 'Ash also said how your father doted on Edwina.'

'It's not news,' Jermaine inserted, realising that Lukas's hesitation must stem from his sensitivity that she might be upset by that fact.

Lukas gave her hands, which he was still holding, a gentle squeeze, and went on, 'I then asked Ash if your father didn't treat you the same as your sister, to which he laughed and said your mother loved you. When I asked, did you love your mother? Ash said your mother had recently had flu and that he'd gained the impression that you'd do anything for her.'

'So you asked him for my parents' address?'

His lips twitched. She loved him. She rather thought she always would. 'Only very casually,' Lukas answered. 'But I didn't have any definite plans to call on them. Only if my business finished early and I was in the right area.'

Jermaine felt her lips twitching too. 'And, hey presto…'

'I had the added information that your mother might still be feeling a shade tired after her flu and, yes, hey presto—it worked like a charm,' he admitted. 'My only problem from then on, sweet Jermaine,' he added softly, 'having been unable to ask your sister to leave without risking a split with my brother, was that when it became apparent that Ash was quickly getting over his infatuation with her I began to fear that *he* would be the one to tell her to go.'

Something in Jermaine began to ice over. 'Because you were starting to grow infatuated with Edwina yourself,' she stated coldly.

'*No!*' Lukas denied vehemently. 'Never in a million years! You daft woman, haven't you seen yet that it's *you* I care about?'

Suddenly her emotions were all haywire again, any ice in her veins going into a rapid thaw. 'M-me?' she stammered. 'You care—about me?'

Lukas stared at her. 'Quite desperately,' he replied quietly.

'Oh,' she whispered, and was too dazed to say anything else.

She wished he would smile, but his expression, as his eyes searched hers, was deadly serious. 'Why otherwise would I be here?' he asked.

Jermaine stared back at him, and all at once she wished he hadn't asked that question. He was here because she had bolted from Highfield. And why had she bolted from his home? Because she had seen him carrying her sister to her bed. The same way he had carried her to her bed last night!

Even while part of her was urging her to give him the benefit of the doubt, Jermaine was attempting to get to her feet. 'No,' Lukas denied her, holding her, anchoring her down. 'You...'

'So tell me about Edwina,' Jermaine cut in. This had happened too many times in the past for her to be able to freely give him the benefit of the doubt. She had been hurt in the past, but never anywhere near as badly as now. Before, it hadn't mattered so much. Now, it did. Lukas meant everything to her. 'Tell me about the love scene I witnessed this morning!' she exploded, barely aware of what she was saying. 'Tell...'

'*Love scene!* Utter rot!' Lukas scorned. 'Hells' bells...' He checked, steadied himself, looking nowhere but into Jermaine's lovely violet eyes. 'I hardly slept. Last night,' he confessed, 'I barely slept at all. Bed became torturous. I was going to see you again, but not until half past eight. I don't know how I got through those sleepless hours—what if I'd got it all wrong? You were different from any other woman I'd known; I knew that. What if, because I wasn't used to anyone like you, I'd misread what I'd imagined were positive signs? What if, because of your innocence, you were giving off the wrong signals?' Lukas halted, then further owned, 'My room became a cage. I left it—quietly, I thought. But Edwina must have heard me, because when, after prowling outside for a while, I came back in and up the stairs, her bedroom door was wide open and she was in a state about some over-large spider on the rampage.'

'She called you in to *catch a spider?*'

'I very much doubt now that there was any such bold arachnid. But at the time I'd got you so much on my mind I thought it best to deal with it quickly—I wanted to be first at our bench. Anyhow, when Edwina fainted, I...'

'Edwina fainted?'

'I thought she had. She appeared to go limp from the shock of seeing the eight-legged animal. It was instinctive to catch her before she hit the carpet. What...?'

Remembering the way her sister had looked directly at her a moment before she'd closed her eyes, Jermaine spoke her thoughts out loud, relief, joy trying to break free. 'Edwina didn't faint.' Lukas hadn't been duplicitous.

'You—sound sure?'

'She does a good faint,' Jermaine answered.

'She's done it before?' Lukas asked, but could see that Jermaine's loyalty was being stretched to the limits, so didn't press her for an answer, but said instead, 'I thought her grip was a bit fierce for somebody who'd passed out. When she wouldn't let go of me after I'd put her on her bed I began to suspect there might be a little play-acting going on there.' He paused, and then revealed, 'She certainly came round pretty quickly when I said I'd get Mrs Dobson to sit with her until she felt better.'

Jermaine had to smile. 'Edwina wouldn't think much of that.'

'I don't think she did, but I'd got other plans. I'd waited for hours to see you, and I couldn't take waiting much longer. No way was I going to call you to hold her hand. To be honest, my dear, if you were going to hold anybody's hand, I wanted it to be mine.'

'Oh,' Jermaine whispered shakily.

Lukas raised her right hand to his lips. 'You believe me, love?' he asked earnestly. 'You believe me that I am not, and never have been, remotely interested in her? Believe my being in her room this morning happened the way I've just said?'

Jermaine knew her sister, knew quite well what she was capable of. It was just that in her adult life she had grown used to male friends deserting when Edwina beckoned.

But Jermaine realised that, as Lukas seemed to think she was different, so she could trust that Lukas was different. She didn't doubt that he knew a lot about women—and began to take in that he had seen through Edwina straight away and had been unimpressed by her. Then it was that Jermaine knew that believe him she did.

But because she was so much in love with him, she owned, it had made her devastatingly vulnerable where Lukas was concerned. Because of past happenings Jermaine still felt on distressingly shaky ground—it seemed impossible that when others had forsaken her for Edwina's charms Lukas was totally immune to them.

'You—um—asked Edwina to stay?' Jermaine reminded him quietly.

For an answer Lukas leaned forward and gently kissed the side of her face. 'It was you I wanted in my home,' he told her softly, and confessed, 'Where at one time I couldn't wait for her to leave, the more I grew attracted to you, the more I realised that if Edwina left you'd leave too. That, in fact, if she wasn't there, you wouldn't come to Highfield at all.'

'You wanted me there?'

'So much. One date with you wasn't enough. One hour with you, two, three, were too quickly passing. I wanted a day with you, two days with you.'

Oh, Lukas. Her heart was pounding. Oh, she did believe him; she did! 'You invited me to stay for Christmas,' she whispered dreamily. 'You invited me to spend Christmas with you.'

'Of course I did. I'd discovered a serious need to see you more and more. Yet I was going away. Lord knew when I would see you again. If you spent Christmas at Highfield, I stood every chance of seeing you on Christmas Eve, the first day of my return.'

Suddenly Jermaine was smiling. 'And when I refused you invited Edwina to stay, thinking—no, not thinking, plotting—that if you came to my parents' home when you were "in the area" on Boxing Day, Edwina might be a lever...'

'In my persuasion to get you to come back with me,' Lukas finished for her, and, looking deeply into her eyes, 'You believe me, Jermaine?' he asked.

She looked back at him, her insides all of a tremble at the warmth and sincerity in his grey eyes. 'I believe you,' she said simply, and felt her bones go weak when the most wonderful smile lit his face.

She thought for a moment that he was going to take her in his arms, but he checked, and instead said, 'Then now, my dear, dear, Jermaine, may we have that discussion which I'd hoped to have several hours ago back at Highfield?'

Jermaine swallowed. 'The—um—one…?'

'The one that began with the two of us meeting, if you cared anything for me,' he encouraged. 'You had intended to be there—at our bench?'

Jermaine smiled a shy smile. 'I couldn't sleep either. I was early leaving my room.'

'Darling,' he breathed, and did then gather her in his arms. 'I love you so much,' he murmured. 'I was at the bench well before eight-thirty. At nine o'clock I bleakly returned to the house, not wanting to believe what I had to believe—that you cared nothing for me.'

'You waited in the cold for over half an hour!' she exclaimed.

'I couldn't believe you wouldn't come hurrying around the corner. Still didn't believe it when I got back to the house. I went up to your room; your case had gone, your belongings had gone—everything except that painting I gave you. It seemed to me then that you had quite clearly given me your answer. But, just as I was starting to despair, Ash rang and said he had you with him and that he had never seen you so upset.'

'You told him to delay getting me back here so as to give you time to get here first?'

'Too true. I told him to drive miles out of his way, call at any house as if he had business there if he had to. I'm sorry, my love,' Lukas said softly, 'but I wasn't ready to admit defeat. I just couldn't, or wouldn't, believe I'd got it so wrong. Arrogant it may be, but, after last night, I just couldn't accept what seemed to be staring me in the face. I chased after you, torn between fury that any woman could make me feel the turned-inside-out way I was feeling—and anxiety in case I lost you.'

Lost her! Her heart was thundering. 'D-did you—um—know you said you—loved me?' she asked huskily.

Lukas, unsmiling, stared into her shy eyes. 'You're embarrassed by my feelings for you?' he asked stiffly.

'Oh, no! No,' she assured him swiftly.

But still he would not smile. 'Then may I take it that, contrary to what you would have had me believe a few hours ago, you do care a little?' he asked tensely.

Jermaine looked solemnly back at him. 'Um—more than a little, actually,' she answered.

Lukas stared at her, unsmiling still, for perhaps about another two seconds. Then, 'Come here,' he ordered—and as he gathered her in his arms she willingly obeyed.

Perhaps five or maybe ten minutes passed while they clung to each other, the pain of parting eased, the anxiety they had endured soothed away. Then gently, tenderly, Lukas kissed her.

'I love you so much,' he breathed. 'Time spent away from you leaves such a void it's like a physical pain. I've felt so empty apart from you.' Jermaine could barely believe her ears, and yet it was all there—his love—in his eyes, his face, his hold. 'You wouldn't mind elucidating a bit on the fact that you care for me "more than a little," I suppose?' he queried, and seemed to be sorely in need to hear more.

Although they were words she'd never spoken before, and she felt shy to utter them, it was because of his need to hear them, that she told Lukas, 'Well, to be honest, the plain truth is—I love you—um—very much.'

'Sweet love!' And with that joyous cry Lukas held her and kissed her, and kissed her and held her. For a short while he seemed content just to hold her close, to glory in being able to hold her this close to his heart as all barriers started to tumble down. 'When?' he asked.

Jermaine drew back. 'Not at first.' She smiled.

'Certainly not at first,' he agreed. 'I wasn't at all nice to you.'

'You were a pig!'

'You're gorgeous.' He grinned, and kissed her. 'When?' he repeated, and she laughed from the pure joy of being with him. Seeing her laugh, he just had to kiss her again.

'When?' *she* asked.

'Cheat,' he replied, but willingly told her, 'Soon after you came to stay that first time, I think.'

'Back then?'

He nodded. 'We were working, yet when always before I've tended to be thoroughly absorbed in my work, I found that Friday with you there in the study with me I was repeatedly losing my concentration. You're so incredibly beautiful, my love, I found I kept looking over to you time and time again.' He kissed the tip of her nose, and smiled as he went on, 'Experience has taught me that outer beauty can hide an inner ugliness, but, given that you'd given me some lip, I just knew that you were beautiful throughout. When I started to get peeved that there seemed to be something going on between you and Ash, I had to face up to it—I was just a tiny bit attracted to you.'

Jermaine's eyes were shining with her love for Lukas as she looked at him. 'Anything between Ash and me was over before I met you,' she said gently.

'I know. I've known for some time.' He hesitated, and then confessed, 'That didn't stop me from being tormented by jealousy again last night when he kissed you.'

'You *were* jealous!' she exclaimed.

'Not for the first time,' he agreed. 'If it wasn't Ash gnawing at my gut, it was your friend Stuart.'

'Stuart!' She had to laugh. 'Stuart's a friend, a work colleague,' she explained. 'We're pals, nothing more.'

'I'm relieved to hear it,' Lukas answered. 'Do you kiss all your work colleagues?' he wanted to know.

'As a matter of fact, I—don't,' she laughed. But sobered to quickly assure him, 'You've absolutely no need to be jealous of Stuart—or Ash either,' she thought she should mention.

'I realise that now. In fact, I knew last night about Ash, when you said that he wanted the two of you to be friends.'

'You did?'

'Ash and I settled matters when I decided I'd have to have a talk with him about you. Only seeing him kiss you last night, as you so rightly guessed, had that green-eyed monster jealousy letting me know what for.'

Jermaine stretched up and kissed him, but pulled back to exclaim, 'You decided to have a talk with him about me?'

'It had to come,' Lukas said. 'It was the last Saturday when you were at Highfield. Ash hadn't known you were coming and said he hoped you weren't dashing back to London. You replied that you were staying to type up the report on my Swedish trip.' At that juncture Lukas stopped, and then asked, 'Are you going to hate me if I tell you what Ash already knew—but you didn't?'

'I hope not,' she answered warily. And pressed cautiously, 'What did Ash know that I didn't?'

'He knew that I'd taken my PA with me to Sweden. Phyllis Gladstone's name is a byword for efficiency. He knew as soon as you mentioned that I'd asked you to type the report on my Swedish trip I was up to something.'

Jermaine owned herself lost. 'Up to something?'

'Oh, dear,' Lukas murmured. 'Confession time is at hand.' Though first he gently kissed her, then pulled back to reveal, 'Don't hate me, sweet love, but Ash instantly knew that Phyllis Gladstone would have had that report already typed and ready for action before we'd even left Sweden.'

Jermaine's mouth dropped open. 'You...? She...? It was already typed?' she questioned incredulously. 'But—but why did you need it typing again?'

'I didn't. What I did need was some time alone with you.'

'You mean...?' Her stunned brain came rapidly awake. 'You're saying you—invented that work...?'

'So I could have your company all to myself without your sister batting her eyes at my wallet, or my brother trying to make off with you.'

'Good heavens!' Jermaine gasped. His lips moved upwards, and she loved him all over again. So she kissed him, was kissed in return, and totally forgot for the moment what they had been talking about. But, suddenly remembering, she recalled, 'You went—that afternoon—you went with Ash to view his new property.'

'I went with Ash because the time to have things out with him could no longer wait.'

'H-have things out with him?' she echoed, faintly staggered that things seemed to have been going on of which she knew nothing.

'My darling girl,' Lukas said softly. 'I'd taken you to an art gallery the evening before, and, watching various emotions cross your lovely face, hearing you laugh your lovely laugh, I started to fall head over heels in love with you. By the time I'd brought you back here, while knowing I had to go away on Monday until Christmas Eve, I was so much in love with you I just couldn't face going away and not seeing you again.'

Her mouth fell open. 'That was when—that night we were having dinner—you'd just swopped your meal with mine because I thought yours looked better, and you laughed—and I fell in love with you,' she confessed.

'Oh, love,' he breathed, and gathered her closer, kissing

her hair. 'Would you have come to Highfield the next day, had I not invented Mrs Dobson needing help?'

Jermaine laughed. 'Of course,' she admitted. But, as she suddenly realised what he was saying, 'You already knew Mrs Dobson had all the help she needed?' she accused.

'Guilty as charged,' he agreed with a smile. Though that smile was totally absent when, going back to his discussion with his brother that Saturday, he explained, 'By the time Ash and I set off, ostensibly to do some house-viewing, all I knew was that I loved you so much that if Ash loved you too this would be one time when I would not be able to assist him all the way.'

'Ash doesn't love me,' Jermaine put in quietly.

'I knew that as soon as he admitted the truth of his behaviour. I'd no idea until he told me that he'd been going out with you *and* succumbing to your sister's charms at the same time.'

'Didn't I say?'

'You know you didn't,' Lukas answered tenderly. 'I can't see you putting the dirt down about either Edwina or Ash. But my anger with him that he could have treated you so was tempered by the fact that, if he could treat you like that, then he certainly didn't love you the heart-and-soul way that I love you.'

'Oh, Lukas,' Jermaine whispered, and received a wonderfully tender kiss in return.

'So, having established that Ash is extremely fond of you, I had his blessing to tell you of my love for you and...'

'You told Ash that you loved me?' she asked surprised.

Lukas nodded. 'He'd guessed—with regard to the *lack* of necessity of you and I spending time alone in my study—that something was going on.' He paused, and then revealed, 'Ash wished me well. You don't hold his behaviour against him? he asked.

'No,' she said simply. 'He was a little gem helping me

today. And,' she added as an afterthought, 'phoning you behind my back to let you know what was going on.'

The both smiled. Smiled and kissed, and kissed some more, holding each other tightly as though wanting nothing to come between them ever again. 'You'll never know the relief it is not to have that jealous demon perched on my shoulder,' Lukas confessed, planting a delicious kiss on the corner of her mouth.

'Er—I've had my jealous moments too,' Jermaine felt honour-bound to confess.

'You have?' he queried delightedly.

'You needn't look so pleased,' she laughed. Lukas loved her. Wasn't that just too wonderful? 'Beverley Marshall,' she announced. 'I thought Beverley was a "she".'

'You felt jealousy before you knew? Back then?' he asked incredulously.

'I wasn't calling it that at the time,' she owned. 'But I thought you were out with some female named Beverley when one night at Highfield I was at dinner but you weren't.'

'It was a Saturday,' Lukas instantly recalled. 'I'd kissed you and, for my sins, was feeling slightly adrift. I didn't like the feeling—I've always been the one in charge,' he inserted self-deprecatingly. 'I decided I needed to get away from you for a while.' Jermaine was still staring at him wide eyed, when he prodded, 'But tell me more.'

'You mean who else was I jealous of besides Beverley? There was Edwina, of course,' she admitted slowly.

His expression grew serious. 'I was never remotely interested in her,' he assured her gravely.'

'I know—now,' Jermaine said quickly. 'It was just that, well, when you phoned her from Sweden...'

'I didn't phone her, I rang Ash,' Lukas cut in. 'Edwina happened to answer the phone.'

Hearing him say that caused Jermaine to wonder why

she hadn't worked that out for herself. Edwina was a past master at hints, evasions and downright untruths. 'I'm sorry,' Jermaine apologised. 'You'd think by now that I'd know better...' She broke off. But when, from loyalty to her sister, she would have left it there, she suddenly realised that from now on Lukas was the most important person in her life, and that because that was so she wanted none of her sister's past barbs and upsets to come between her and the man Jermaine loved. 'I've been...'

'You've been, my darling?' Lukas encouraged.

'A fool, mainly,' she admitted. 'Getting all stewed up that you kissed me that Friday when you returned from Sweden but then went home to Edwina. When, since she was a guest in your home, where else would she be? Even if it was late when you arrived back at Highfield...'

'And found Edwina lying in wait, as it were. Sorry, sweetheart, I know she's your sister, but you're the one I'm going to marry, and I'm not having you upset...' He broke off at the stunned look on Jermaine's face. 'What?' he questioned urgently. 'What...?'

'Do you know what you've just said?' she gasped.

'Explaining about having to be nice to your sister because she is just that—your sister? I'm sorry, my love, but I can spot a money-grabber from a mile off. I don't want to hurt you, sweet love, but I want nothing to cloud what we have. I want you to know exactly how it was—is—with me. How I've been love-sick to see you. How I wanted quite desperately to phone you while I was away the last time, only to discover that—having never been in love before—my self-confidence had taken such a hammering I was scared to ring in case the call went all wrong, and I'd be left stuck overseas feeling even worse and more love-sick than ever.'

'Oh!' Jermaine gasped on a whisper of sound. Dared she

believe she was hearing what she was hearing; had she heard what she thought she had heard?

'My dear love,' he went on tenderly, 'I was hoping with all I had that you'd come back to Highfield with me yesterday—Mrs Dobson has been on red alert to have your room ready ever since I knew where my heart lay.'

Jermaine's eyes were saucer wide. 'Oh!' she gasped faintly again.

'Christmas Day was the worst of my life,' he went on to reveal. 'I wanted you with me, and, since that hadn't happened, I wanted no other company. Edwina was my guest, but I found there was only so much of her wittering I could take. So I prevailed on Ash to keep her company while I shut myself in my study and planned various courses of action if you refused to come back with me the next day.'

'Oh, Lukas,' Jermaine sighed.

'Jermaine,' he murmured, and kissed her, and confessed, 'And when, glory of glories, you did come back with me, I started to get all chewed up that if Edwina left you wouldn't see any reason to say on at Highfield either.'

'So you asked her to stay as long as she liked,' Jermaine put in, her heart racing.

'I don't think I put it quite like that, but since it was *you* I wanted in my home I might well have gone over the top a bit in my bid to get closer to you—to have you with me for ever.'

For ever! Her heart did not merely race, it jumped and sped, and her throat went dry. 'Er...' she tried.

'What?' Lukas pressed when she seemed stuck for words. 'You know you can tell me anything, ask me anything—we are as one now.'

Oh, my heavens! *As one!* 'I—er—well, did you say what I thought you said?'

'Tell me,' he said urgently. 'If I've said something wrong, I'll mend...'

'You said something about marrying me, and...' His stunned expression caused her to break off, and she went scarlet. 'I'm sorry,' she said quickly. 'I misheard.' She went to stand up, but Lukas had no intention of letting her go.

'There's nothing wrong with your hearing,' he swiftly let her know.

'You're shocked?'

'True,' he agreed, holding her fast when again she tried to get away. 'But only because I've just realised that, as proposals go, I didn't do that very well. Forgive me, my darling,' urged. 'There's been such a welter of anxiety within me, a need to clear away all misunderstandings—a need, basically, to get you to be willing to see me as a suitor—that I've missed the most important part.' Tenderly, then, Lukas looked into her wide violet eyes. 'I love you so much, Jermaine,' he told her quietly. 'And you've said that you love me. So am I hoping for too much, do you think, by asking you to marry me?'

She had never felt so fluttery inside. 'No,' she answered, unable to bear his tense expression as he waited. But, suddenly unsure if that should have been a yes, 'I mean, no, you aren't asking too much,' she added quickly.

But Lukas did not smile. 'Then, will you, Jermaine Hargreaves, marry me?' he asked.

She smiled, because she loved him. 'I'd be honoured,' she answered, and was pulled against his thundering heart for long, long seconds. Then, tenderly, he kissed her

'Thank you, my darling,' he breathed, and for an age just sat feasting his eyes on her, until, holding her close and still looking deeply into her eyes. 'I feel I want to shout the news that you've agreed to marry me from the rooftops. May I start by ringing Ash and telling him, my love, that Santa did bring me what I most wanted, after all?'

**What happens when you suddenly discover your happy twosome is about to be turned into a...*family?*
Do you laugh?
Do you cry?
Or...do you get married?**

The answer is all of the above—and plenty more!

Share the laughter and the tears with
Harlequin Romance® as these
unsuspecting couples have to be

When parenthood takes you by surprise!

THE BACHELOR'S BABY
Liz Fielding (August, #3666)

CLAIMING HIS BABY
Rebecca Winters (October, #3673)

HER HIRED HUSBAND
Renee Roszel (December, #3681)

Available wherever Harlequin books are sold.

Visit us at www.eHarlequin.com   HRREADY2

Harlequin invites you to walk down the aisle...

To honor our year long celebration of weddings, we are offering an exciting opportunity for you to own the Harlequin Bride Doll. Handcrafted in fine bisque porcelain, the wedding doll is dressed for her wedding day in a cream satin gown accented by lace trim. She carries an exquisite traditional bridal bouquet and wears a cathedral-length dotted Swiss veil. Embroidered flowers cascade down her lace overskirt to the scalloped hemline; underneath all is a multi-layered crinoline.

Join us in our celebration of weddings by sending away for your own Harlequin Bride Doll. This doll regularly retails for $74.95 U.S./approx. $108.68 CDN. One doll per household. Requests must be received no later than December 31, 2001. Offer good while quantities of gifts last. Please allow 6-8 weeks for delivery. Offer good in the U.S. and Canada only. Become part of this exciting offer!

Simply complete the order form and mail to:
"A Walk Down the Aisle"

IN U.S.A	IN CANADA
P.O. Box 9057	P.O. Box 622
3010 Walden Ave.	Fort Erie, Ontario
Buffalo, NY 14269-9057	L2A 5X3

Enclosed are eight (8) proofs of purchase found in the last pages of every specially marked Harlequin series book and $3.75 check or money order (for postage and handling). Please send my Harlequin Bride Doll to:

Name (PLEASE PRINT)

Address   Apt. #

City   State/Prov.   Zip/Postal Code

Account # (if applicable)   **097 KIK DAEW**

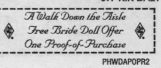

HARLEQUIN®
Makes any time special®

Visit us at www.eHarlequin.com

A Walk Down the Aisle
Free Bride Doll Offer
One Proof-of-Purchase

PHWDAPOPR2